Dark London

An Anthology

Volume Two

www.darkstroke.com

Discover us online:
www.darkstroke.com

Find us on instagram:
www.instagram.com/darkstrokebooks

Include **#darkstroke** in a photo of yourself
holding his book on Instagram and
something nice will happen.

This volume is dedicated to the soul of London, which permeates everyone and everything around it.

Thank you

Thank you for purchasing the second volume in the Dark London Anthology.

All royalties received will be split and donated to two London-based charities, The London Community Foundation, and Centrepoint.

The publisher is grateful to those who have contributed to the publication of the Anthology. Their work has been done without payment.

Please consider purchasing Volume One in the Dark London Anthology – available in paperback and on Kindle across Amazon.

Dark London

An Anthology

Volume Two

Foreword

Mark Patton

"*It was the best of times, it was the worst of times, it was the age of wisdom, it was the age of foolishness, it was the epoch of belief, it was the epoch of incredulity, it was the season of Light, it was the season of Darkness, it was the spring of hope, it was the winter of despair, we had everything before us, we had nothing before us, we were all going direct to Heaven, we were all going direct the other way – in short, the period was so far like the present period, that some of its noisiest authorities insisted on its being received, for good or for evil, in the superlative degree of comparison only.*" (Charles Dickens, *A Tale of Two Cities*, 1859).

Charles Dickens's *A Tale of Two Cities* was written at a time when London and Paris, the two cities of the title, were probably the largest cities in the world, with populations of around 2.8 and 1.9 million respectively. By 1900, London was, incontestably, the largest city on Earth, with a population of 6.5-6.6 million, a position that it retained until around 1925, when it was overtaken by New York. Today, one must venture far beyond the continent of Europe to glimpse anything remotely comparable to this rapid urban expansion. I have seen, heard, felt, tasted, and smelled it on the streets of Guangzhou and Shanghai, in China, where mazes of narrow alleys, with four storey wooden buildings, lit by gas, were being demolished, even as I explored them, to make way for the shopping malls and neon lights of the modern megacity, now twice the size of London.

Such times of change (and London had seen several such in the two thousand years before Charles Dickens was born) were always seasons of light, and springs of hope, for some; and winters of despair for others. Social mobility, the prospect of which attracted both foreign refugees, and the sons and daughters of country folk in their millions, operated in both directions, and at an alarming speed: as we see, for example, in William Hogarth's two series of paintings, *The Harlot's Progress* (1731-32), the originals of which have been lost; and *The Rake's Progress* (1732-35), now in Sir John Soane's Museum. It was always possible to make one's fortune in London, as Sir Richard ("Dick") Whittington (a real man, who served four terms as Lord Mayor in the early 15th Century) did; but it was equally possible to lose everything, and to end one's days in the squalor of the workhouse or the asylum, like Hogarth's fictional characters, Moll Hackabout and Tom Rakewell. Bad decisions may have played a role in many such declines, but so did bad luck, as William Hogarth, a generous benefactor of London's Foundling Hospital, understood only too well. Poverty; infectious disease; mental illness; crime & the punishment of it; and addiction to drink, drugs, & gambling; all played their part in defining the 'dark side' of London's identity as a city, which has provided so much material for poets, novelists, playwrights, and artists, throughout the course of London's history.

So, too, has the proximity, within the City of London, especially, of the world of the living, and that of the dead. The modern 'City', centred on Saint Paul's Cathedral and the Bank of England, is built directly on top of the Medieval City (largely destroyed in the Great Fire of 1666), which, in turn, is built directly on top of the Saxon City (planned by Alfred the Great), which, in turn, sits on the ruins of the Roman City of Londinium, established shortly after the Emperor Claudius's invasion of Britain in 43 AD. Whenever a major building development is undertaken within the City (as recently, for example, at One New Change, just to the east of Saint Paul's), a palimpsest of archaeological remains is revealed, with Victorian and Georgian cess-pits cutting through medieval foundations and the mosaic floors of

4

Roman houses and administrative buildings. Even the business letters of Medieval Londoners (including the deeds of sale of an unfortunate slave girl named Fortunata) have been found beneath the modern streets. When we walk through 'The City', from Newgate to Aldgate, or from London Bridge to Bishopsgate, we walk along streets that would have been familiar to Geoffrey Chaucer, William Shakespeare, and John Milton, even though few of the buildings that they knew have survived: the street names, alone, bearing testament to their former character (Bread Street, Milk Street, Honey Lane, Poultry).

Whilst the Romans, motivated as much by superstition as by hygiene, insisted on the burial of the dead beyond the limits of their cities, the urban populations of the Middle Ages preferred to keep their dead relatives close to their dwellings, as well as close to their hearts. London before the Great Fire had no fewer than one hundred parish churches, each of which had bodies buried in the crypt or beneath the floor, and in the surrounding churchyard. By the beginning of the nineteenth century, these burial grounds were literally overflowing with corpses, and at least one grave-digger was asphyxiated by the noxious fumes rising up from the soil in which he was working, prompting a return to the Roman practice of burial at a distance, and the establishment, between 1832 and 1841, of London's 'big seven' suburban cemeteries (Kensall Green, West Norwood, Highgate, Abney Park, Nunhead, Brompton and Tower Hamlets).

With the living and the dead crammed into such close proximity with one another, it is unsurprising that, in the older parts of the capital (including Southwark, Lambeth, Westminster, Camden, and Tower Hamlets, as well as The City), there is scarcely a street or a pub without an accompanying ghost story, providing an additional, supernatural, element to the idea of London's 'dark side'. Indeed, London could be seen as the birthplace of 'The Gothic': the original 'Gothic novel', Horace Walpole's *The Castle of Otranto* (1764), with its ghost emerging from an ancestral portrait, being based on his residence at Strawberry

Hill, Twickenham.

There is little hint of London's 'dark side' in the earliest substantial description of the city that has survived, written by a cleric, William FitzStephen, in 1190, and included as part of the introduction to his biography of his martyred colleague and friend, Thomas Becket (it is reproduced in John Stow's (1598) *Survey of London* (a key document for anyone who wishes to understand London's history). FitzStephen was probably, like Becket, a Londoner, and was keen to emphasise the light, rather than the darkness, positioning the city as a centre of learning and religious devotion. There is at least a hint of this 'dark side', however, in John Lydgate's poem, *London Lickpenny*:

"Then unto London I did me hie,
Of all the land it beareth the prize.
"Hot peascods!" one began to cry,
"Strawberry ripe!" and "Cherries in the rise!"
One bade me come near and buy some spice,
Pepper and saffron they gan me bede,
But for lack of Money I might not speed...
...Then into Cornhill anon I yode,
Where was much stolen gear among;
I saw where hung mine owne hood
That I had lost among the throng:
To buy my own hood I thought it wrong;
I knew it well as I did my Creed,
But for lack of Money I could not speed."

Lydgate, a contemporary of Geoffrey Chaucer and Sir Richard Whittington, was a Benedictine monk, who presents the capital as a place where a countryman (his family was from Suffolk) might, almost literally, lose his shirt to thieves and conmen.

It is, perhaps, surprising, that two of England's most famous literary figures, Geoffrey Chaucer and William Shakespeare, both of whom spent a large part of their lives in London, have so little to tell us about the life (dark or otherwise) of the capital. Shakespeare, in the Henry IV plays, gives us some vignettes of the boisterous life of a London tavern (The Boar's Head in Eastcheap, demolished in 1829); whilst his friend and sometime rival, Ben Jonson, in comic plays such as *The Isle of Dogs* (1597), *The Alchemist* (1610); and *Bartholomew Fair* (1614) satirises the greed, pretensions, and self-importance of London's merchant classes. None of these gentle satires, however, really amount to an exploration of London's 'dark side': for this, we have to wait for the 18th century, where, once again, we find ourselves in the world of William Hogarth.

What Hogarth contributed to the visual arts was matched, in literary terms, by John Gay. Originally from Barnstaple, in Devon, Gay spent most of his working life in London, where he was a close associate of the poet, Alexander Pope, and the satirist, Jonathan Swift. His (1716) *Trivia, or the Art of Walking the Streets of London* was yet another gentle satire on middle- and upper-class urban *mores*, but his (1728) *Beggar's Opera* went much further. The character of Mr. Peachum was ostensibly based on the real-life example of Jonathan Wild, who had a double role as thief-taker, and as a receiver of stolen goods, but was also seen as a direct parody of the notoriously corrupt Prime Minister, Robert Walpole (the father, incidentally, of the Gothic novelist, Horace).

The central message of the play was that corruption and dishonesty were the organising principles of commercial and political life in London at the time, and that this was as true of the Prime Minister, and of society lawyers and leading churchmen, as it was of the highwaymen and prostitutes who made up the cast of the play itself.

Peachum: "*Through all the Employments of Life*
Each Neighbour abuses his Brother;
Whore and Rogue they call Husband and Wife:
All Professions be-rogue one another:
The Priest calls the Lawyer a Cheat,
The Lawyer be-knaves the Divine:
And the Statesman, because he's so great,

Thinks his Trade as honest as mine.

A Lawyer is an honest Employment, so is mine. Like me too he acts in a double Capacity, both against Rogues and for 'em; for 'tis but fitting that we should protect and encourage Cheats, since we live by them."

The Beggar's Opera ran for sixty-two consecutive performances, making it the greatest commercial success on the London stage to date. At a time when George Frideric Handel was at the height of his powers, writing Italian operas to be sung in London by Italian celebrity performers to aristocratic and high bourgeois audiences in packed houses, here was an entertainment for the masses, in effect, the fore-runner of today's West End musicals. What makes it truly an exploration of London's 'dark side', however, was the context of the criminal justice system of the time, characterised by later historians as the 'Bloody Code'. The number of crimes punishable by death increased from fifty, in 1688, to two hundred and twenty, at the end of the 18th century, largely in response to a perceived epidemic of crime, especially in London. At the heart of *The Beggar's Opera* is a recognition of profound injustice: corruption is revealed as a near-universal feature of society, but, whilst this brings nothing more than mild disgrace to the rich and powerful, the poor must pay with their lives for their smallest misdemeanours, a sentiment expressed, in the play, by the condemned highwayman, MacHeath:

"Since Laws were made for ev'ry Degree,
To curb Vice in others, as well as me,
I wonder we han't better Company,
Upon Tyburn *Tree!*
But Gold from Law can take out the Sting;
And if rich Men like us were to swing,
'Twou'd thin the Land, such Numbers to string
Upon Tyburn *Tree!"*

The 'Bloody Code' was ended by the Judgement of Death Act (1823), greatly reducing the number of offences for which execution was the automatic or default penalty, and this was followed, in 1868, by the abolition of public executions in England.

In a broader sense, however, it can hardly be a coincidence that the literary exploration of London's 'dark side' flourished at precisely the time at which the nature of the city itself was changing. London in Chaucer's lifetime had a population of 40-50,000, one of many such cities in Europe at the time, and the equivalent of a relatively small town by today's standards. In Shakespeare's time, it had risen to 200,000, which was similarly unremarkable by European standards. It passed the one million mark in around 1800, at a time when Beijing, at around 1.1 million, was the largest city on Earth. The only cities that might ever have been larger than this were Rome in the 3rd Century AD, and Baghdad in the 11th and 12th Centuries AD (1.2 million, in both cases, according to some estimates, although this is by no means certain).

Already, by 1794, when William Blake published his *Songs of Experience*, the human cost of this expansion was becoming apparent:

"*I wander thro' each charter'd street,*
Near where the charter'd Thames does flow.
And mark in every face I meet
Marks of weakness, marks of woe.

In every cry of every Man,
In every Infants cry of fear,
In every voice: in every ban,
The mind-forg'd manacles I hear

How the Chimney-sweepers cry
Every blackning Church appalls,
And the hapless Soldiers sigh
Runs in blood down Palace walls

But most thro' midnight streets I hear
How the youthful Harlots curse
Blasts the new-born Infants tear
And blights with plagues the Marriage hearse."

By 1859, when Charles Dickens published *A Tale of Two Cities*, London's population, still rapidly growing, exceeded 2.8 million. Nobody on earth had ever known what it was like to live in a city of more than three million, but it was clear that London would inevitably be that city within a few short years. The consequences of this expansion were already being felt: major cholera epidemics struck London in 1832, 1848, 1853-4, and 1866; and, in the summer of 1858, the 'Great Stink', occasioned by the volume of sewage in the Thames, finally spurred the public authorities into action. The London relief sewers, built between 1859 and 1875, under the supervision of the engineer, Sir Joseph Bazalgette, ended this particular chapter of London's dark history.

The state had, by this time, stepped back from the direct role that it had taken, under the 'Bloody Code', as the executioner of great numbers of the poorest Londoners, but was increasingly reluctant to intervene to challenge even the worst excesses of poverty and deprivation. Reformers insisted that "something should be done," but there was no general agreement on what that something might be. Some considered the despair of the poor as an inevitable, if unfortunate, consequence of modern life, to be chipped away at through paternalistic benevolence; or even as a 'price worth paying' for the extraordinary growth of the British economy, the sufferings of the weak weighed in the balance against the prosperity of the strong.

A Tale of Two Cities is one of only two historical novels by Dickens (the other being *Barnaby Rudge*). Most of his novels deal with the problems and circumstances of his day, and the majority are set wholly, or partly, in London. These problems and circumstances, including child cruelty and exploitation (*Oliver Twist* & *Nicholas Nickleby* – 1839); the Poor Law & workhouses (*Oliver Twist*); the physical impacts of industrialisation, and of London's expansion (*Dombey & Son* – 1847); and the inhumanity of the penal system, even after the end of the 'Bloody Code' (*Little Dorrit* – 1857, *Great Expectations* – 1861); largely define 'Dark London' in the mid-nineteenth century, and Dickens was, without doubt, the pre-eminent author of them. Dickens did not see it as part of his role, as a writer, to propose solutions to the problems that he highlighted: indeed, he was suspicious of simple solutions, whether they took the form of political reforms, as proposed by the Chartists in the 1840s, or structural economic change, as proposed by Friedrich Engels and other Socialists. However much he invites us to sympathise with the plight of his downwardly mobile characters, he also makes it clear that many of them, such as Wilkins Micawber in *David Copperfield*, are, at least in part, the authors of their own misfortunes. This, for Dickens, was viscerally personal, since he applied that judgement, most especially, to his own downwardly mobile, and ultimately bankrupt, father. If he envisaged any solution to the darkness that he witnessed during his insomnia-fuelled night-time walks through the streets of London, it was straightforwardly more of 'the milk of human kindness', as in *A Christmas Carol* (1843).

A less moralistic observer (although he does not deny the role that such factors as drinking and gambling sometimes played in the process of downward mobility) was Henry Mayhew, whose *London Labour and the London Poor* (1851), a work of journalism rather than fiction, drew attention to the most marginalised people in London society, including those who eked out a precarious living as 'mudlarks' (a term first recorded in 1796, although it may have been in popular usage before this), collecting pieces of coal, bone, and fabric in the mud of the Thames foreshore. The lives of these 'mudlarks' had previously been dramatised in Frederick Marryat's (1842) novel, *Poor Jack*, which is not widely read today, although it is actually in print. Today's 'mudlarks' still walk the foreshore, but in search of archaeological finds, rather than a means of subsistence.

The beginning of the end for the appalling conditions of

life and work lamented by William Blake, Charles Dickens, and Henry Mayhew alike came with the first elections to the newly established London County Council in 1889. Nineteen years earlier, the Elementary Education Act had created free school places for all English and Welsh children between the ages of five and twelve. In 1889, many of the young adults who had benefitted from this education had the vote (more specifically, many of the young men, since women could not yet vote in local or parliamentary elections): the election was fought, not between Liberals and Conservatives (as Parliamentary elections were), but between Progressives and Moderates; the former being an alliance between radical liberals, inspired by the 'municipal socialism' of Joseph Chamberlain in Birmingham, and Fabians, including Sidney and Beatrice Webb, who would go on to found the Labour Party. The Progressive victory of 1889 ushered in a new agenda of social housing, public services (water, gas, ultimately electricity), and the 'betterment' of public infrastructure, at least in the capital.

Even as this election victory was being planned, however, a new chapter in London's dark history was opening. The murders of five women in and around Whitechapel, in the autumn of 1888, gave renewed impetus to the idea that the world's greatest and most rapidly expanding metropolis had a dark underbelly. The victims came from precisely the downwardly mobile sections of London society that Charles Dickens, and before him, John Gay, had written about, but, in a city in which violent crime had long been rife, these murders attracted the public attention as few crimes before them had ever done. They were, in many ways, the first serial killings of the modern mass-media age, the press reports enlivened by speculations about the identity of 'Jack the Ripper' (the epithet itself coming from one of many letters written to the Police and press, claiming to be from the killer), and the fact that the murders remain unsolved even down to the present day can only add to the mystique of the case.

London today, with an estimated population of around

11-15 million, barely counts as a 'megacity' at all, compared to Tokyo (38 million), Delhi (26.5 million), Shanghai (24.5 million), or Mumbai (21.4 million). Like all major cities, it has its 'dark side': its poverty and squalor; its criminal underworld; vice; homelessness; even people smuggling and 'modern slavery'. It is no different, in this, from Manchester or Edinburgh, let alone Istanbul or Moscow, yet the idea of 'Dark London' endures, not least because London is still London, and we walk the same streets that John Gay and Charles Dickens walked, and all that has happened in those streets since the time of William FitzStephen and Geoffrey Chaucer remains part of who we are, as Londoners. Our streets have developed organically, in ways that the modern streets I strolled along, in Guangzhou and Shanghai, have not. We may no longer keep the bodies of our dead as close to our homes as Medieval Londoners did, but their spirits haunt the very streets and stones of the city. I cannot walk along Milk Street, without imagining the Crespin family, Jewish merchants who lived there in the 13th century, and whose ritual bath we can see at Camden's Jewish Museum; or enter Saint Helen's Church, in Bishopsgate, without thinking of William Shakespeare, who was once a parishioner there; or come up the escalator from the underground station at Bank, without remembering the Roman slave-girl, Fortunata, whose home must have been close by. Jim Crace, one of our greatest living novelists, spoke of the English landscape as being 'drenched in narrative': he had in mind a rural landscape, to the north of London, which inspired his poetic novel, *Harvest*, but the urban landscape which I have now called home for most of my adult life is no less drenched in narrative, and there is poetry here, too.

The twentieth century has given us new lenses through which to see the World, including distinctive genres of fiction. When Charles Dickens sat down to write *A Tale of Two Cities*, and *Barnaby Rudge,* he chose to set those novels against the background of events (the French Revolution, and the Gordon Riots, respectively) that had taken place before his birth, but it is difficult to imagine that he thought of himself as writing 'historical fiction', since the category did not really emerge until the twentieth century, although, retrospectively, we may assign a number of earlier works to this category, including *A Tale of Two Cities*, and *Barnaby Rudge*, but also (for example) Daniel Defoe's (1722) *Journal of the Plague Year*. Twentieth century novels that explore aspects of 'Dark London' include Bruce Holsinger's (2014) novel, *A Burnable Book*, a tale of intrigue and murder in the time of Chaucer; Ros Barber's (2012) *The Marlowe Papers*, and Peter Ackroyd's (1994) *The House of Doctor Dee,* which explore similar themes in the context of Elizabethan England, with an added supernatural element in Ackroyd's case; and Jake Arnott's (2017) *The Fatal Tree*, exploring, from a modern perspective, the consequences of the 18th century 'Bloody Code'.

If London is a city 'drenched in narrative', then this must surely include the narratives currently being written, and those yet to be written, as well as those that we have inherited from the past. Anyone embarking on a literary career with a knowledge of, and passion for, London, as part of his or her background, will find enough material for a lifetime of writing in the London Metropolitan Archives at Clerkenwell, perhaps even starting with their own family history, but with any number of digressions along the way, in the manner of *Tristram Shandy*. The stories in this volume, some of them historical, others contemporary; some of them exploring the grim realities of poverty and crime; others delving into the dark mysteries of the uncanny, and the supernatural; are contributions to this process of becoming; recognitions that London, dark or otherwise, its past, as much as its present or its future, is a city always in the process of becoming; and a city that has always existed, and will always exist, in the human imagination, as well as on the banks of the Thames. This London of the mind has never been the exclusive property of Londoners, although anyone, whatever his or her background, can become a Londoner.

By way of conclusion, here is *The Lights of London*, a poem by Louise Imogen Guiney, a 19th century American visitor to London:

"The evenfall, so slow on hills, hath shot
Far down into the valley's cold extreme,
Untimely midnight; spire and roof and stream
Like fleeing specters, shudder and are not.
The Hampstead hollies, from their sylvan plot
Yet cloudless, lean to watch as in a dream,
From chaos climb with many a sudden gleam,
London, one moment fallen and forgot.

Her booths begin to flare; and gases bright
Prick door and window; all her streets obscure
Sparkle and swarm with nothing true nor sure,
Full as a marsh of mist and winking light;
Heaven thickens over, Heaven that cannot cure
Her tear by day, her fevered smile by night."

———————————

 **Mark Patton** was born on Jersey, and studied Archaeology and Anthropology at Cambridge, before completing his PhD at University College London. He has taught at the universities of Leiden, Paris 1, Wales, Greenwich, and Westminster, and currently teaches for The Open University.

He is the author of three historical novels, as well as a number of academic books and journal articles in the fields of archaeology, history, and historical biography.

Treading

Angela Wren

The Silent Highway wove through the heart of the city, an early morning damp smog swirling above the rippling and lapping waters as the tide reached its zenith. At its fullest, the surface water was churned and disturbed by barges, lighters, tugs, wherries, and ships bringing freight. All the river traffic was belching steam and coal smoke, adding to the dense atmosphere that spewed onto the wharves and the narrow streets beyond, lined with row after row of cramped terraced houses. At high tide, the water was anything but silent.

"Come on, son. We'll be late."

Thomas Clements' heavy boots clattered down the bare wooden steps as he fixed his flat cap firmly in place and pulled the peak well down. At the bottom of the stairs, he glanced from his father to his grandfather and back again.

"Ready, Pa."

"Remember, if anyone asks, you're fourteen."

Thomas nodded as his father, John, tugged at the door. The three of them stepped out into the heavy September mist that clung to the houses and streets of Southwark.

The sound of boots on the pavement, dulled by the damp, was accompanied by a low murmur as groups of men and their sons made their way to the commercial docks. Thomas could feel his finger-ends beginning to go numb. This late in the month, the early morning air had a bite to it. On the embankment, more men were making their way to the warehouses in the hope of work. As his father and

17

grandfather strode out through the crowd, Thomas quickened his pace. He couldn't afford to lose sight of them. Not today. Not now the strike had been settled, and he was going to be doing a man's job – proper men's work instead of marking. Marking was for boys. With the dock gates in sight, the mood of the crowd changed. Men jostled to the front. In the distance, Thomas could just make out the cry of a ganger calling for coal backers. "A filthy, back-breaking job," his grandfather had said.

"Watch it!" Thomas grabbed at his cap as a man pushed past him from behind. He repositioned the worn, second-hand headgear and threaded his way through.

"Pa?"

His father turned. "Keep close to me, boy. Keep close."

Not quite as tall as his father but just matching his grandfather's height if he stretched his spine, Thomas slipped between his relatives and waited. Around him, men were smoking the last of their gaspers and crushing them out on the cobbled surface underfoot. Gangers were calling for daymen to clear the goods from the wharves into the warehouses. Thomas waited along with around forty other men who wanted employment as deal porters. He looked at his father, who remained still, staring towards the dock buildings and the wharves. A small man, dark-haired and with an uneven gait, walked into the yard, and Thomas sensed his father's dislike.

"Damn it! It's Cullen." John clenched his left fist and slapped it into the palm of his right hand.

"Calling on. Deal Porters, I'm calling Deal Porters for the Baltic Cross. Deal Porters for the Baltic Cross."

Thomas saw the sneer on Cullen's face as the ganger looked directly at his father. Cullen stepped forward, name book in hand and shouted, "Calling on. Deal Porters for the Baltic Cross."

"Keep close by me and pull your cap well down," said John as he shepherded his son forward.

Cullen reeled off a list of names. "…Gardiner, Jefferson, Kilcoyne and Clements. James Clements." He glared at John as he uttered the last name and Thomas noticed his father's jaw tighten.

James nodded and doffed his cap. "Thank you, Mr. Cullen." He turned to his son. "Leave the boy with me, John. I'll show him."

Thomas stared at his father. Waiting. Hoping.

"Alright."

Thomas let out a breath.

"Look after him," said John. "I can't lose another one, Pa, and you know what Cullen's like."

James nodded and followed after Cullen, pulling his grandson along with him.

"Mr. Cullen, I've my grandson with me, Sir. He's here to port, Sir."

Cullen stopped and turned, a sneer on his face. "Grandson?" He swaggered across the yard. "Young Thomas, is it? Don't reckon you've portered before?"

Thomas felt his grandfather's dig in the back of his ribs.

"I'm fourteen, and I learn quick," he blurted out. His bravado soon disappeared. The hairs on the back of his neck began to prickle as Cullen looked him up and down. He swallowed hard.

"He's a bit small for his age. He'll only port half a load. He's no use to me. He can mark instead." Cullen turned to walk away.

"But Pa said—"

The vice-like grip of his grandfather's gnarled hand on his shoulder silenced Thomas. Cullen spun around and snapped his ledger shut.

"Spirited, is he? He didn't get that from his feckless father." Cullen focused his attention on James. "Half a load, half the pay. Tuppence ha'penny an hour." Cullen strode off.

"Mr. Cullen," James raised his voice but didn't go after the ganger. "Half the load, half the pay. That's fair. We don't want trouble, Mr. Cullen. We just want work. So, half the load, half the pay is very fair, Sir. But it'll be threepence for the lad, Mr. Cullen. It's what was agreed by the strike committee. Sixpence an hour for me and the other men, so that'll be threepence an hour for the lad."

Thomas watched as his grandfather stood straight, his thumbs in his waistcoat pockets, his gaze never leaving Cullen. Thomas waited.

"Get to the wharf!" Cullen stalked away. "And take that wretch with you," he shouted without looking back.

Thomas followed his grandfather. Men were already at work, long turns of deal on their shoulders. Thomas pulled his leather shoulder shield from his pocket. It had been his older brother's, and it didn't fit that well, but it would do for today. Once he got his first pay, he promised himself he would put a little aside and save enough to get a shield of his own.

"Check the marks and remember to call," said James. "Watch what I do and follow me."

In silence Thomas strode behind his grandfather. At the edge of the wharf were vast piles of timber with dual walkways of planks in-between – one for the men carrying the wood and one for the men returning for another load.

"Just one for the boy," said James, nodding to the worker at one end of the stack of deal. "I'll take my usual." James turned, and with the help of another docker, he took the load of timber and shouldered it. He let out a long breath and straightened his back.

"Watch me and do what I do, lad. Find the rhythm of the plank, Tom. You'll keep your balance if you find the rhythm."

Thomas saw the strain in the old man's face, noticed the left arm held out for balance as his grandfather moved forward at a slow, steady trot. With help, Thomas took his turn of wood. It was heavier than he thought and, in an effort to take the weight before he had the balance of the load, he almost sent the timber crashing to the ground.

"Steady, boy," said the man helping him shoulder the load.

Thomas moved gingerly along the walkway. He glanced ahead only to see James disappearing onto a downward plank, the stretch of wood receding through the air. Thomas quickened his tread, the wood underfoot flexing as he tried to keep an even steady pace. As he stood at the start of the downward plank, he heard his grandfather's shouted instructions to keep the right distance as he walked from the wharf to the vast warehouse.

"Move, lad." Another porter was almost directly behind him, and Thomas stepped onto the next plank, hardly daring to breathe and with a knot in his stomach.

"Keep it steady, boy," said one of the other porters as they passed each other at the threshold of the warehouse.

Thomas stopped and watched his grandfather. The turn of planks steady on his shoulder, the smooth tread of his feet through the wood dust on the floor. The air smelled of trees edged with the sweetness of pine and sap. As the men moved, the atmosphere shifted. The sound of slapping planks as they were stacked on the registered owner's pile reverberated throughout the vast space only interrupted by the calls of the men navigating the narrow wooden walkways supported by trestles and other previously stacked lengths of deal.

"Walk with the rhythm, lad," shouted James as he stepped onto a new plank. "Treading," he bellowed to the man behind, who slowed his pace until the walkway was clear. James placed his turn and moved along the pile of timber to the down walkway. Standing aside, he watched as Thomas ascended with his load.

"Shout, boy!"

The late morning sun, having burned through the smog, warmed and dried the sweat on the back of Thomas' shirt. He bit into the chunk of bread that his mother had given him. It wasn't that fresh, but he didn't want to eat it all at once. There would be more work soon. Another vessel had already pulled alongside, and the final loads of timber were being stacked on the wharf.

"Right, lad, we need to get back to work." James downed the last of his porter and wiped his hand across his forehead. Getting up, he stood for a moment. Thomas smiled as the old man put his hands on his haunches and stretched his back. It was something he'd seen his grandfather do many times.

21

Thomas followed as James strode out across to the warehouse.

"Shirking, Clements?"

Thomas spun around, his heart in his mouth. The voice seemed to be in his ear. Cullen stood right in front of him. He took a step back.

"No, Sir. Just waiting for the signal to start porting, Sir."

Cullen grinned. "Is that right?" He shifted his balance onto his back foot; arms folded across his chest and stared at Thomas. "How old did you say you were?"

"Fourteen, Sir."

Cullen snorted. "So that'd make you, how many months younger than your dead brother?"

Thomas frowned. "I don't—"

"Come here, lad," shouted James, a turn on his right shoulder. "Get to work."

Thomas sprinted across to the pile of deal. Fixing his shield, he took a deep breath. This time the churning in his stomach wasn't hunger. Thomas shouldered his turn. He took a breath and paused. Another deep breath and he had his balance and his confidence. He trotted to the warehouse. As he was about to place his foot on the first walkway, he shouted his intention to tread. Moving with the spring of the plank, he ascended to the first level. On he went along the walkways until he stood twenty feet above the floor of the warehouse. His turn in place, raw pain in his tired shoulder, Thomas walked back to the wharf for another.

The relentless trudge to and from the wharf to the warehouse continued into the afternoon. Thomas' back was aching. His whole body seemed to be screeching with pain and, when one of the other porters stood aside to allow him the honour of porting the last turn, Thomas could feel the last reserve of his energy beginning to drain away. He glanced at his grandfather. The old man's face was grey with sweat and weariness.

"Go on, lad. It's the last of the day." James sat down on a wharf-side bollard, his elbows on his thighs. He let his head and shoulders slump forwards. Thomas braced himself and took the timber. The pain in his shoulder screamed under the weight. As he crossed the wharf the muscles in his thighs tensed, the burn traversed upwards through his legs to his spine. Every breath, every step fuelling the fire of exertion. He wanted to be home. He wanted his man's work to be over. Inside the warehouse, he stopped at the first walkway and looked up and opened his mouth to shout.

"No need for that, Clements," said Cullen as he rounded the pile of timber. "There are just us here."

Thomas took a breath. "Yes, Sir." He placed his foot on the walkway and then another. Feeling the flex of the plank, and keeping his balance, he began to trot.

"Fancy yourself as a Blondin, do you, Clements?"

Thomas could hear the mockery in Cullen's voice. He kept his focus on his balance and the top of the walkway and continued, one step at a time. He felt a shift in the rhythm of the plank and stopped.

"We were interrupted earlier, Clements. Now, you were going to tell me how many months difference in age there were between you and your older brother."

Thomas froze. *What do I say?* He shifted the turn on his shoulder. *Grandpa!* He took a deep breath and continued onto the next walkway. *Don't think about it.* He took the final few steps. The plank was tipped onto the pile of deal and landed with a clap. The relief to his aching muscles was immediate as he slowly rolled his shoulders and stretched his back.

"I asked a question, Clements, and I expect an answer if you want me to keep giving you work."

Thomas tried to contain a smile. "He was fourteen, Sir, the same age as I am now." Hands in his trouser pockets, Thomas sidled down the walkways. As he reached the floor of the warehouse, Cullen was on him, grabbing his right arm and pulling it back and up towards his shoulder. Thomas screeched.

"That's wiped the insolent smile off your face, Clements, hasn't it?" Cullen relaxed his grip a little. "That brother of yours. In May, when he last worked here, he was fourteen.

23

That's four months ago. You're here, and it's September, and you say you're fourteen."

"I am. I'm fourteen, Sir." Thomas wriggled to get his arm free, but Cullen's grip was like iron. "I'm fourteen," he spat out, his face scarlet with effort and rage.

"He's right, Mr. Cullen." James Clements appeared at the entrance to the warehouse. Standing straight, he watched and waited.

Cullen glared and shoved Thomas to one side.

"The men are waiting for their pay, Mr. Cullen."

The ganger strode across to James and stood toe to toe. "They'll get paid when I say they'll get paid and that little bastard of a grandson of yours is getting his money docked for answering back." Cullen swept out onto the wharf.

Thomas left his grandfather in The Porter's Arms and headed along the narrow streets to his home. A dim light came from the window of number 11.

"Ma, it's me." He walked into the single room at the front.

Franny Clements, her shawl gathered around her shoulders, was rocking her youngest child's cradle with her foot as she encouraged her five-year-old daughter, Frances, to eat. Thomas tipped his day's earnings onto the table. "Grandpa's at the Porter's," he said, slumping down onto the only available chair at the small table. "He's talking to that lighterman again and said he'd be home after he's finished his glass of ale."

Franny handed the last of the heel of bread to Frances and began to count the coins.

"…Seven, eight." Franny frowned and shoved the coppers around as she recounted them. "One and eight! Is that all they'd pay you for a full day's work?"

"It was Cullen," said Thomas.

"Cullen?" She pulled Frances onto her knee. "Was it old man Cullen or his son, William?"

"I don't know. But Pa didn't like him when he saw him."

Franny looked at her son and secured a stray lock of hair behind her ear. "William Cullen, then." She nodded and pursed her lips. "He's a mean, evil man." She scraped up the money and put it in a small tobacco tin she kept in the pocket of her apron. "There's some broth," she said, freeing her wriggling daughter. She leaned across to stir the contents of the pot on the fire. "Leave some for your elders."

Thomas nodded and grabbed a dish from the table. In seconds he had the hot broth brimming to the top of the bowl.

"Thomas." His mother's sharp tone was enough, and he tipped half of it back as the front door slammed shut.

"Franny, is Pa back yet?" John Clements stood in the doorway, his face black with coal dust and his clothes smelling of sweat and carbon.

"Grandpa's at the Porter's," said Thomas, barely lifting his head from the task of eating. "He's talking to that lighterman again," he said between spoonfuls. Scraping the bowl clean, Thomas shoved his dish away. "Pa, why did Mr. Cullen keep asking about Edward?" Thomas frowned. The look that passed between his parents seemed to mean something. He just didn't know quite what.

"What was he asking?"

"How many months difference in age between Ed and me." Thomas bit his lip and looked from one parent to the other.

"You shouldn't have told him to lie, John. I told you not to tell him to lie." Franny sat up straight, letting the cradle come to a slow and gentle stop. "Cullen's worked it out. I knew he would."

The glare that his mother directed at John was not lost on Thomas. *So, that talk about Cullen on the docks today was right then.* As soon as the thought formed in his mind, he shook it from his head. This was his mother. *No, it can't be right.*

"Worked out what, Ma?" Thomas stared at her.

"That's no matter. Tell me exactly what Cullen said," John had taken a step back and, feet apart, his hands resting on each side of his waist, he seemed to have commandeered all the space in the room.

"Just that, if Ed was fourteen when he died in May, then I

couldn't be the same age now." Thomas looked at his parents; his father's glare was turning into anger. Thomas knew that steel of a look in his pa's eyes. He'd been on the receiving end of his father's wrath more than once.

"It's not his fault, John," said Franny, pulling her shawl tight around her shoulders. "Never you mind, Tom. It's between me and your—"

"We've got him!" James Clements shouted from the front door as he burst in. "We've got Cullen." He stepped into the tension in the room. Thomas watched. The colour in his grandfather's cheeks drained as he glanced around at his family. The front door clamped shut behind him, and the baby let out a wail.

In the grey, early morning light, three generations of the Clements family rounded the corner of the street onto the main thoroughfare leading to the embankment and the docks. Thomas had to stride out to keep pace with his elders. *Pa's got something on his mind.* Thomas fell back a little and looked at his father's straight shoulders, head held high. His mother's whispered words, just as they left the house a short while ago, echoed through his thoughts. *It must be about Mr. Cullen.* That had to be it, he decided. *But what?* Breaking into a trot to catch up, he promised himself that he would keep quiet and let his elders deal with things. Just like his mother had said. *It's best to leave it to Grandpa.*

At the dock gates, too many men to count were milling around. The constant thrum of noise from the river, accompanied by the bad swirling air, made Thomas uneasy. His father stood to one side of the main body of the crowd. His eyes were hooded, his cap pulled down partially masking the look of thunder on his face. Thomas stood close to his grandfather.

"It's alright, lad. Me and your father have got an old score to settle." The old man winked.

Thomas sniffed. *I'm not a kid anymore.* He flexed his shoulders, but his grandfather wasn't looking. Both his elders were watching William Cullen as he strode towards the crowd, and Thomas shifted his gaze.

"Deal porters for the Norway Star," shouted Cullen. "Calling deal porters…" He began to rattle off a list of names as he had done the day before.

Thomas waited to see if he would be called. But only other men were afforded the privilege of work that day. As the called men moved towards the wharf, Thomas saw his father stride up to Cullen, but his grandfather held back.

"Me and my father are here to work, Mr. Cullen," said John. "So is my son, Thomas." John swept his cap off his head and beckoned his son. Thomas took a couple of paces forward.

Cullen stood with his ledger under his arm and a broad smile across his face. "So you want me to give you work do you, John Clements?"

Thomas stared at the ganger. There was something false about his look. It was in the eyes. *You don't mean that smile, do you, Mr. Cullen?* Thomas looked at his feet and shoved his hands in his trouser pockets.

"Yes, Mr. Cullen. I'm a good worker, you know I am. I've worked for you before."

"You have, Clements. But that was before the strike. Today's today. And today it's different."

"Mr. Cullen, I've had no work since the strike was settled. That's nearly two weeks with no money. Soon the deal ships will stop sailing. I must get some work, Mr. Cullen, before winter sets in."

"There's no work here for you."

"Please, Mr. Cullen. I can port more deal in an hour than any of the men you've already called on. I can port more goods than my own father. You know that. We must have work today, Mr. Cullen. I owe on the rent, and we've no food."

"There's no work here. Not for trouble-makers like you." Cullen turned and walked away.

John set off after him, but James grabbed his arm.

"Don't beg, son. He's not worth it. We'll try the other wharves. There'll be other work."

"Yes. But not necessarily at sixpence an hour."

Thomas shook his head. *Labouring's hard, and that's all I'll get.* He let out a sigh. The status afforded deal porters was something he had craved for a long time. He looked across the river and thought about his brother, Edward. He fought back a wave of emotion as he reminded himself that it was his brother's accident on the wharf that had provided him with the opportunity to port deal.

"Thomas," his father shouted. "We'll try the other wharves, and we can deal with Cullen later."

Thomas nodded and trotted after the two men.

The Porter's Arms was busy as always at the end of a day's work. In one corner of the bar, Mr. Cullen was transacting business. Over by the full window was the lighterman and his sons that had been talking to his grandfather the day before.

Thomas and his elders were leaning against the bar. *How much longer do we have to wait?* Thomas looked around. Cullen was still talking to someone. Thomas slumped down onto a nearby stool. His stomach began to churn, and he shoved his hands in his pockets and tried not to think about how hungry he was.

"Cullen's shut his ledger," said John.

Thomas looked across the room. Both the men stood and shook hands across the small round table. *That'll be the price for tomorrow's work agreed, I suppose.* Thomas got up and followed his elders across to the corner where Cullen now sat alone.

"Mr. Cullen, we'd like a word if you've got a moment, Sir," said James as he took the stool directly opposite. John took the only other available seat, effectively blocking the ganger in the corner of the settle and preventing him from leaving. Unsure what to do, Thomas remained standing between them.

"If it's about this morning's work allocation, then I haven't time." Cullen rose to his feet, his ledger under his arm and glared at the three of them.

"No, Mr. Cullen. We want to talk about my grandson, Edward," said James as he got out his pipe, penknife, tobacco and vesta case. Each item was carefully laid out on the table in readiness for the paced ritual of preparing a smoke. Thomas found the process fascinating. One of his earliest memories as a child was watching his grandfather fill his pipe. He undertook each action in precisely the same way every single time. *Why do you do that, Grandpa?* Thomas grinned as James scraped the bottom of the pipe bowl with the penknife and blew out the offending debris.

"You see, Mr. Cullen, no matter what the Coroner said at the inquest, I know my grandson's accident was not quite as it was presented at the time of the enquiry." James pocketed his penknife and turned his attention to his tobacco.

Cullen shifted his stance. "I don't know what you're talking about. The Coroner has ruled that—"

"Sit down," hissed John. Thomas flinched at his father's tone. He knew what that meant.

"You see, Mr. Cullen, I, we, now know that there was someone else in the warehouse when Edward fell," said James as he carefully pushed the threads of tobacco into the bowl of the pipe.

"What?" Thomas shot a glance at his father. *But it was an accident.* He was on the verge of verbalising his thought when his grandfather shushed him. The glacial stare was enough. *How does he always know what I'm thinking?* Thomas sighed and waited.

"Now, just a minute—" Cullen was on his feet again.

"No, Mr. Cullen, *you* wait a minute."

Thomas held his breath and looked across the table at his father. John's sole focus was the ganger.

"We've been talking to a lighterman and his sons," said James, striking the vesta into light and applying the flame to his pipe.

"And your point is what, Clements?" Cullen thumped his ledger on the table and leaned towards James, his eyes narrowed, his tone sharp.

"Just that what was actually seen wasn't what was

reported to the Coroner." Thomas kept his eyes on Cullen who sniffed, his face as thin and mean-looking as it had been all morning.

"You've got nothing on me, James Clements. Get out of my sight and take your kin with you. None of you will get work on the port again. I'll make sure of that."

"Oh, will you now? Just remember one thing, Mister Cullen, I know you were in the warehouse when my grandson Edward died. You were seen."

Cullen let out a roar of laughter. "Ha! Is that it? Some lies you've heard from some riverman, Clements. That won't help you."

James grinned. "I think it will." He chewed the end of his pipe. "This particular lighterman has four sons. It was high tide, and two of them were on the wharf, making ready to secure the vessel for unloading. The youngest was sent to look for you, Mr. Cullen."

Cullen's face changed in an instant as he slowly sank back onto the settle. Thomas watched as his grandfather stared across the table at his adversary.

"He saw what you did. He saw you follow Edward up to the third level. He saw you dislodge the walkway when Edward was halfway along."

The skin on Cullen's face was ashen. Thomas clenched his fists. *Don't, leave it to Grandpa.* He tried to blink his growing anger away.

"Nothing to say, Mr. Cullen?" James took a long draw on his pipe.

So, that's what Ma meant. Thomas shifted his gaze to his father. John's jaw was tight set; he was staring at Cullen and remained stock-still.

"But that's not the first time there's been an accident like that on your watch, is it, Mr. Cullen?"

"I'm not listening to this nonsense, Clements." Cullen stood. "Get out of my way!" He grabbed the table and tried to push it to one side. John and James were too quick for him, and between them, they shoved the table back and into Cullen, effectively pinning him down on the settle. They shifted their seats forward.

Thomas felt his heart thumping against the wall of his chest. He took a step back. *Leave it to Grandpa.* His mother's advice was playing through his mind like a mantra.

"I know men at Katharine docks, Mr. Cullen. I know all about the little accident involving your father-in-law from a few years ago. Couldn't work after his accident. Could he, Mr. Cullen? Your father-in-law was so badly injured from the accident that he could barely do any sort of dock work."

"Mind your own business," Cullen snapped.

"But you bettered yourself, didn't you? Because it was you who got his ticket and regular work."

Thomas wanted to shout. The pounding in his ears was deafening. *Leave it to Grandpa.* He shoved his hands in his pockets. He had to be sure he didn't lash out. He caught his grandfather's eye. The look and the slight nod were enough.

"And who caused that accident, Mr. Cullen? Eh? Does your wife know the truth? The real truth?"

A tense silence hung in their corner of the bar. James smoked his pipe, John sat braced as if ready to pounce, and Thomas watched and waited.

It was James who broke the tension. "There's also the deliberate treading while Thomas here was on the walkway, yesterday."

"Grandpa!" The single word providing a moment of relief for Thomas. *But that means...* Thomas shook his head. *Why?* He wanted to shout it out.

"Shush, lad." The even but commanding tone and the look on his grandfather's face quelled Thomas' need. Just.

"I don't know what you mean."

"Yes, you do, Mr. Cullen." James took a long draw on his pipe and exhaled, adding blue smoke to the already dense atmosphere. "Of course, silence has a price, as I'm sure you know."

Thomas watched as the faint flicker of a self-satisfied smile ghosted across his grandfather's face. It was an echo of the look he always adopted when, at the end of a full day's work, a meal in his stomach, he would sit in silence with his pipe.

Cullen shifted in his seat. "What's your price?"

"Work, Mr. Cullen. Regular work for me and John and day work for Thomas."

"I've got enough preferable men on my books already."

James stood and bent over the table. "I'll just go and get a constable."

"No! Wait." Cullen opened his ledger and scanned through the pages. "There's work tomorrow, and I can call you on as preferable men."

James stood up straight, his thumbs in his waistcoat pockets. "That's a start. But we want permanent work, Mr. Cullen."

"That'll mean working in the warehouse once the deal ships stop running."

James grinned. "Just so long as we understand each other, Mr. Cullen." James stepped back and nodded to John. "Thomas, come on, lad." James turned to walk away.

Thomas hesitated as his father pushed his chair away from the table and moved towards Cullen.

"Just one last thing," said John as he grabbed Cullen by his coat. "Tread where my son Thomas is treading, and I will tread you into that river. I will tread you so deep in the Thames that not even the mudlarks will find you."

"John, that's enough." James was back at the table in an instant. "That's enough, John. Calm down!" James had his strong hand on John's bicep.

Thomas was rooted to the spot, his heart racing. Under pressure from James, John released his grip on Cullen.

"Tomorrow, Mr. Cullen. John, come away. We've got what we came for." Thomas moved back from the table and waited. His father and grandfather nodded to each other and turned away.

Thomas followed. When he glanced back, Cullen slumped on the settle, his coat awry and his trembling hands barely able to pick up his ledger.

Bibliography

Various documents from the archives at the Docklands Museum, London
The Story of the Dockers' Strike, 1889. H. Llewellyn Smith & Vaughan Nash
The Book of the Thames. Mr. & Mrs. S. C. Hall
Wonderful London. Ed. St. John Adcock

Angela Wren is an actor and director at a small theatre a few miles from where she lives in the county of Yorkshire in the UK. She worked as a project and business change manager – very pressured and very demanding – but she managed to escape, and now she writes books.

She has always loved stories and story-telling, so it seemed a natural progression, to her, to try her hand at writing, starting with short stories. Her first published story was in an anthology, which was put together by the magazine 'Ireland's Own' in 2011. She also works with 8 other northern writers to create the series of Miss Moonshine anthologies.

Angela particularly enjoys the challenge of plotting and planning different genres of work. Her short stories vary between contemporary romance, memoir, mystery, and historical. She also writes comic flash-fiction and has drafted two one-act plays that have been recorded for local radio.

Her full-length stories are set in France, where she likes to spend as much time as possible each year.

Follow Angela's Blog: **www.angelawren.co.uk**

The Night Bus

Chris Dommett

Jambo! Let me introduce myself. My name is John. John Waka. But I don't exist, officially.

I am from Kenya, but tonight this is my home: back seat, top deck, Route N8. The London Night Bus from Oxford Circus to Hainault. Ninety minutes each way, ten minutes turn around, result: over three hours of interrupted sleep. But warm, familiar, and much safer than sleeping rough.

Tonight, though, I am scared. It's not the usual mild anxiety; drunk and rowdy fellow passengers, young skinheads looking for fun, sadistic bus drivers insisting that I leave the bus at its Hainault terminal. No, those are part of my life. Tonight is different.

Let me go back into the past to explain why I am here, and scared.

I was once a respected manager of a small bank branch north of Mombasa. All was going well until I fell foul of the coast mafia by doing the right thing. They left me for dead among the sharks of the Indian Ocean. Maybe that is a story for another day. I escaped and made my way to England where I applied for asylum. Two years later, my asylum request denied and appeals exhausted, I was issued with a Deportation Order. I was to be sent back to Kenya – and certain death.

I was prepared for this. While going through the process I had come in contact with many in the same position, and they all had the same advice: disappear.

So I did. I left my accommodation, lived rough, and joined the swarm of anonymous faces drifting through London's underbelly. I slept under bridges, ate when I could at soup kitchens, rummaged in bins for cast-off clothing, and never registered my name anywhere.

My daily goal was survival; staying safe, staying unnoticed, staying alive. But I also had a longer term strategy. After two years pleading for asylum, if I could somehow avoid deportation for another eighteen years, I could legitimately apply for the Leave to Remain in Britain. I had done my homework while waiting for the appeal verdict. Twenty years in the UK (excluding any jail time) and I could apply, whether my stay was 'lawful' or 'unlawful'.

I had become a true outlaw.

And that is why I now spend every night riding the London Night Buses, but not why I am so scared tonight. Kenya is a real but distant memory, while my fear is very much of the present.

The Night Buses are an integral part of London life and I fit right in. I have an Oyster Card in someone else's name which I top up each month, either from what I can earn doing odd jobs for cash, or from a very kind lady at an East End charity. She is smart enough to know that most cash given to the homeless ends up in booze, ciggies or drugs, so she prefers to donate for something more useful.

Among the shift workers returning home, office workers who missed the last train after too long in the pub, travellers heading for the airport, and the general insomniacs, no-one notices the black guy hunched against the window of the back seat. They get on, they get off, sing, shout, drink, sleep, occasionally throw up, but usually just ignore me. And that is how I like it.

I vary my routes to avoid attention. Occasionally a bus driver will recognize me as a regular and give me a cursory nod as I cause no trouble and always swipe my card. Most buses start and finish either in Trafalgar Square or Oxford Circus, so I head there at around midnight after finding something to eat. I tend to avoid the shorter journeys, and those which stay mainly in Central London. Too many passengers getting on and off, and too many bright lights disturbing my sleep.

The N8 is my favourite. For much of the way it trundles through East London and into Essex, mainly dropping passengers off. The stops become less frequent once we leave London, and there are longer stretches of darkness as it becomes more rural. It is also one of the longer routes, so two round trips and that's it for another night. After nearly eighteen years of this life, only fifty-two nights remain for me to survive before I can officially exist again.

I think I'm going to make it. Or at least I did until strange things started happening about a month ago.

That's when I noticed that a couple of other 'regulars' were no longer following their usual routines as our paths crossed. At first I thought nothing of it. I recognize most of the deportation dodgers. We all have our preferred buses, and we often chat as we wait at the Night Bus stops in Central London. Some are new to this life and keen to swap tips on which buses to avoid and where you can find a decent free meal. Others like me are veterans of many years, hardened by our experiences, reluctant to talk in case we give too much of ourselves away.

We never swap names. It is safer that way. I know the two missing 'regulars' as Tall Nigerian and Quiet Chinese. They both favoured the West London routes. Fewer drunks and less hassle, they claimed. They would sometimes join me on the Hainault bus, but we would not sit together. A group of sleepers would attract attention, and they left me the back seat, top deck out of respect for my age, I guess.

First to disappear was Quiet Chinese. A short man with an ageless face, he always seemed to be reading a Chinese book through his thick spectacle lenses. I spoke to him briefly before we boarded the N8 in Oxford Circus, both eager for the dry warmth of the bus after waiting in the driving rain. I took my usual seat at the back, while he chose somewhere halfway to the front, seeking anonymity.

I quickly dozed off, oblivious to other passengers and the sights of London. At Stratford station I was woken by the drunken singing of a few city boys, but they staggered off at Gants Hill, leaving me to return to my doze. Only a few of us were left on the upper deck, but I could see the head of Quiet Chinese propped against a window several rows ahead of me.

I woke next as we left Barkingside, and he was gone. This was unusual. Perhaps he needed a piss. If so, he would no doubt rejoin the bus as it returned. I hoped he could find somewhere dry to shelter while he waited.

I looked out for him twenty-five minutes later as we stopped in Barkingside, but no sign of him. I knew he had disembarked somewhere between Gants Hill and Barkingside, but no Quiet Chinese to be seen.

I assumed he had found a decent place to spend the night and looked out for him over the next few days in Oxford Circus. I even asked some of the 'regulars' if they had seen him. Nothing.

Perhaps he had found a way out of our dire existence? A successful asylum appeal? A place to stay? A generous benefactor? I feared the worst, and scanned the newspapers scavenged on the buses for news of an unidentified body turning up somewhere in darkest Essex. Still nothing.

Two weeks later Tall Nigerian joined me in the N8 queue. Darker than me, he had a soft, deep voice, and bore his height with a grace that suggested a previous athleticism. He was always smartly dressed, with a dark blue suit under his long raincoat, and an old-fashioned homburg on his head. We exchanged familiar nods as we boarded the bus, and both made for our preferred seats on the upper deck after swiping our Oyster cards.

The journey took its usual course as we collected the Night Owls of Central and East London, and I drifted in and out of sleep. At Stratford I noticed three black guys taking the seats just behind Tall Nigerian who was slumped forward against the seat in front, fast asleep.

I dozed off again and woke as the bus started its climb up Fencepiece Road after Fullwell Cross. I saw the backs of the group as they made their way forward towards the stairs of the bus. One of them was being supported by his mates and was clearly in no state to make his way safely off the bus. At Neville Road the bus stopped to let them off. As we resumed our journey, I watched them stagger towards a white van parked just off the main road in a side street, but soon lost sight of them. I looked back as the bus gathered speed and glimpsed a fourth man turning down the side street.

I realised then that Tall Nigerian was no longer in his seat.

Should I get off at the next stop and double back to check he was OK? Or keep my head down and avoid trouble, serving my time until I could become a person again?

I procrastinated long enough to make the first option redundant, but as we waited in Hainault, I resolved to get off at Neville Road on the way back, just in case. There should be another bus along in half an hour, and I felt I owed it to my fellow struggler.

As the bus approached the stop, I had serious second thoughts. I would be risking my years surviving off the grid as well as possibly my personal safety. I am not a brave or stupid man, but something pushed me to act.

I stepped off the bus when it stopped, and hearing the doors swish shut behind me, took a deep breath. I would start by looking up the side street for the white van, and then widen my search for Tall Nigerian in the surrounding area. Thirty minutes maximum and then back on the next bus, due at 2.02am.

There was no sign of the van in Neville Road, nor in Kingsley Road – just rows of smart suburban houses, with an assortment of cars parked outside. I headed back towards Fullwell Cross, passing more houses with an occasional glimpse of dark, grassy expanses of playing fields and woods on my left. It was too dark to see anything beyond the road, and by the time I reached the roundabout at Fullwell Cross I could see the lights of the N8 making its return to London.

Safely back in my usual seat I was far too shaken to sleep. Should I report Tall Nigerian's disappearance, even anonymously? How would I explain it without giving myself away? How would the Police react to a report of a non-existent man without a name being dragged from a London bus?

No, I would wait a few days. Maybe there was a good explanation for the two 'regulars' going missing. I wasn't going to risk everything at this stage.

Days passed, and still no sign or word of Tall Nigerian or Quiet Chinese. I tried different Night Bus routes, heading West rather than East, without success. I asked other 'regulars' but they all assumed the missing guys had somehow made it into the system.

For many homeless people like myself London's Public Libraries are a Godsend. They provide warmth and shelter during the day, but also access to information. I decided to do some research, looking for a possible explanation for the disappearances. An internet search for charitable organizations in the Barkingside area drew a blank so I consulted Google Maps to see what else might have drawn them from the Night Bus.

From the satellite view I saw neat rows of houses, but also cricket pitches, golf courses and the green expanse of Fairlop Waters Country Park. This is border country where the urban expanse of London meets Green Belt and the wilds of rural Essex. Ancient woodlands like Epping and Hainault Forests stand within easy walking distance of Central Line Tube stations, with house prices to match.

Clearly, this was no obvious place for the two men to hide.

Let it drop, or do something about it? The last time I was faced with such a dilemma I had done the 'right' thing, and look where it got me!

But I couldn't let it drop. I felt an affinity with these two men, though I hardly knew them. Like me, they were outlaws. No one cared if they existed. I had to do something, even if just to salve my own conscience.

With plenty of time to kill every day I decided to visit the area in daylight. Perhaps by exploring on foot I could find something. Next day I broke the habit of many years and boarded a regular bus in daytime. The world of London looked very different. More crowded, noisier, but somehow greyer and drearier than by night.

I was drawn towards Fairlop Waters, and alighted from the bus at Fairlop Tube station. A short walk along Forest Road brought me to the entrance to the park, where I sat down on a bench to consider how best to approach my search.

Well frequented areas like the golf course, kids' playgrounds and car parks seemed unlikely. If Quiet Chinese or Tall Nigerian had ended up there, no doubt someone would have found them, dead or alive. There is a large island in the middle of the Waters, but with no means of reaching it other than swimming, I left that for another day.

A track circles the lake, and I set off, scanning the ground to either side of the path for any signs of the two men. I nodded a greeting to the occasional dog walker or jogger I passed, but I didn't see anything out of place.

At the far side of the Waters there is a car park, and I left the path to have a look around. No white vans parked conveniently nearby, but I did spot some faint tyre tracks leading away from the car park across the grass towards a smaller, more secluded pond.

I followed these almost to the water's edge where they stopped in a thicket of trees. The tyre tracks deepened as the ground became damp, and it looked like the vehicle had struggled for grip as it started back for the car park.

There were some footprints in the soft mud, but these could have been made by an angler or birdwatcher. I widened my search to the bushes bordering the pond.

A battered homburg. A pair of cracked spectacles. And finally, a small Chinese paperback book.

That is why I am scared tonight. I need to see those black men again. I will risk my freedom, and even my own safety, if it means I can give the police more than just a story and a collection of discarded personal items.

The plan is to stay awake for the whole return journey, and if the men get on, then I will try to photograph them secretly with my very basic Nokia phone camera. I won't accost them. I am not brave enough for that. My phone is an anonymous pre-paid 'burner', and I will send the photos to the police with a message explaining what has happened and what they will find at Fairlop Waters.

This is the fifth night since my discovery, and each night I have repeated my usual journey on the first N8 from Oxford Circus. Each night, fortified by the rare luxury of a cup of coffee, I have kept my vigil, expecting the men to appear at every stop between Gants Hill and Hainault.

As I board the bus I recognize one of the more friendly drivers who greets me with a cheery "Ev'nin', mate," as I swipe my card.

"Ev'nin'," I reply with a nod. I never say any more than that to the drivers. Over the years, I have acquired a mild London accent to mask my Kenyan lilt; I'm trying to blend in.

I am sitting in my usual seat. I can see everyone who climbs to the upper deck, assessing them for anything unusual or threatening. We pass through Holborn, Bank and into the East End: Shoreditch, Bethnal Green and on towards Bow and Stratford. There is always plenty of activity at Stratford, and I think back to the energy and goodwill emanating from this area during the London Olympics in the summer of 2012. The world had been welcomed here then. For a few brief weeks I felt like a person again, admitting to anyone who asked that I am Kenyan, proud of my country and its athletes.

But now I can't indulge in such happy memories. I need to stay focused.

At Stratford three white men take their seats a few rows ahead of me. Eastern Europeans, I think. I am looking for the black guys and pay them no attention as they huddle together in conversation.

As we leave the large Redbridge roundabout and head along Eastern Avenue towards Gants Hill one of the men stands up and walks back to the seat just in front of me. He has a scarred face and is scruffily dressed, but appears friendly, or at least non-hostile. He sits down and leans back conspiratorially towards me.

"How long to Hainault?" he asks, his accent thick and slightly slurred.

I don't want to talk, but also eager to avoid any confrontation.

"About twenty minutes," I reply.

He turns back to face the front. As the bus approaches Fullwell Cross one of his companions joins him. The second man turns to me: "What time now?" His accent is stronger than the first man's.

"One twenty," I reply.

"Show me," he says, pointing at my watch.

I reach forward to show him when he grabs my arm, and I feel a sharp stab in my bicep.

There is something hard and wet against my cheek. I hear loud voices shouting. Someone is shaking me, but I struggle to open my eyes. When I manage this, I see a blue tie and a white shirt with a badge on it. I focus on the bus driver from the N8 who is leaning over me and shaking me.

"Thank God!" he says. "You OK, mate? I thought they 'ad you there."

I mutter something incoherent even to me.

"OK, you stay 'ere," he replies. "I need to get back to the bus and call the police. You'll be fine now. They buggered off in that white van when they saw they'd been clocked."

"What happened?" I manage to ask before he can disappear.

"Well, I spotted these Albanian geezers gettin' on and thought they looked like trouble. So when they come down the stairs carryin' you I knew something wern't right. I was too slow closin' the doors on 'em so I jumped out and legged it after 'em. They saw me runnin' and shoutin', and I guess that spooked 'em so they just dumped you on the pavement and shot off in their van. Lucky escape for you, I reckon."

He props me up against a garden wall, and lumbers back towards the brightly lit bus still blocking the end of the side road. I have to think quickly. Stay until the police arrive or

43

try to get away? I manage to sit upright, but my legs won't respond. Instead a wave of nausea hits me and I throw up my coffee on the wet pavement. The decision is made for me. I'm not going anywhere at the moment.

The N8 has moved from the end of the road to let a police car enter, its blue lights flashing. I'm aware that my worst fear is about to be realised, but I don't care. I don't know what awaited me in the white van, but even a warm, dry cell would surely be better.

An Indian policeman is first out of the car. "Can you tell me what happened, sir? Are you OK?"

"Attacked. Three men," I mumble.

"OK, just hang in there. The medics are on their way," he reassures me, and turns away to talk into his shoulder radio.

The paramedics arrive a couple of minutes later. I show no physical signs of an attack, so they only have the bus driver's word that I am not simply drunk. They check my neck and eyes for serious damage before loading me into the ambulance on a stretcher.

At the hospital I am wheeled to a triage station for an examination, but the only mark is a swelling on my left bicep. I still can't move my legs, so the doctor takes some blood for some tests. They decide to keep me in overnight. Luxury – a warm bed for the night.

I wake in the morning for the doctor's visit. He explains that while there appears no lasting damage, they have found strong traces of Ketamine in my blood sample. This would explain my temporary paralysis. I can now move my legs again. After taking my blood pressure and pulse the doctor pronounces me well enough to speak to the police officer waiting outside my cubicle.

I recognize the Indian guy from last night. He introduces himself as P.C. Singh and starts with a tough one. "Name and address, please, sir?"

I take the plunge and tell the truth. "John Waka. No fixed address."

"And originally from…?" he asks.

"Kenya."

"Legally here, sir?"

A long pause while I consider how much to tell him. "Asylum seeker," I reply eventually.

"OK, let's hear what you can remember about last night's attack. I'll decide later if Immigration needs to get involved. Sounds like the bus driver did you a really good turn, though. He's given us his side of things so we have some sort of picture but tell me everything you can."

So I do. I skim over my arrival in UK, my failed request for asylum, and my disappearance into the world of Night Buses. But I give him everything I can remember about the vanishing men, my attempts to find them, the personal items at Fairlop Waters, and the events of last night.

When I finish, the policeman looks down at his notes. "Can you be more specific on the dates the two men disappeared? If so, we can check the CCTV on the buses and maybe get a look at the abductors."

I can be very specific. Dates, times, and in the case of Tall Nigerian, an exact location. I also describe the two men in as much detail as possible.

"OK, sir. That should be enough for now, but I'm going to need you down at Barkingside Police Station to make a formal statement. And don't even think about disappearing again, or I'll have the Immigration boys down on you like a ton of bricks."

I agree to be at the police station at ten, and he leaves me to get dressed. Apart from a slight soreness on my left bicep I actually feel fine, physically, but still badly shaken by my near miss with the white van gang. I sign myself out of the hospital and, realising that I haven't eaten much since yesterday lunchtime, I head for a small café.

I know Barkingside Police Station well. The N8 stops there every night. It's my first time inside, though, and I present myself at ten sharp to the Duty Sergeant at the front desk.

"John Waka," I announce myself, feeling strange at the sound of my own name, so rarely spoken. "I've come to give

45

a statement."

The sergeant consults a clipboard, then picks up a phone. A brief inaudible conversation, and he asks me to take a seat. I sit feeling uncomfortable for what seems like an age, but in reality is only about ten minutes, before P.C. Singh appears and leads me to an interview room. A detective in a well-tailored suit is waiting there, and all three of us sit down across a table dominated by a large recording machine.

P.C. Singh turns on the machine which gives out a long piercing bleep.

"Interview with John Waka of No Fixed Abode on 14th May 2019 at 10.15am. D.I. Allan Moore and P.C. Parvinder Singh in attendance," announces the smart detective for the benefit of the tape. We then go over the same ground I covered at the hospital, with D.I. Moore occasionally asking a question to clarify a point.

At first his questions seem sceptical. How can I be certain that the two men have been abducted? Why didn't I come to the police earlier? Why did I choose Fairlop Waters for my search? Once we get to the events of last night, he appears more convinced. P.C. Singh gives the bus driver's version and confirms the doctor's report of finding traces of Ketamine in my blood sample.

Finally, Moore leans back in his chair, tapping a pencil against the table. "OK Mr. Waka. We're going to need you to stay here while we get hold of the CCTV footage from the buses. If that checks out, we're going to need you with us when we go to Fairlop Waters with a forensics team. You'll be safer here as well. If these guys are who we think they are, you're a marked man."

Turning to P.C. Singh, he added, "Better get some protection for the bus driver as well. I doubt they could I.D. him, but they might have someone in TfL who could check the rosters."

The two policemen leave, and the Duty Sergeant leads me down some stairs to a cell.

"Am I under arrest?" I ask him.

"No, sir, but unfortunately our Royal Suite is under

renovation at the moment," he replies with heavy sarcasm.

And so, after almost twenty years of some sort of freedom I am finally in a jail cell. To be honest, it doesn't bother me as much as I thought it would. At least it is safe. I lie down on the bed and fall asleep.

I wake to the clanking of the cell door in late afternoon. D.I. Moore beckons me out. "We're going on a nature ramble to Fairlop Waters," he explains as we walk down the corridor and up the stairs. "The CCTV checked out."

A short ride in an unmarked police car and we reach the car park at the Hainault end of Fairlop Waters. We wait a couple of minutes for the forensics team to arrive, then I lead them through the trees to the edge of the smaller pond. I point out the tyre tracks and the bushes where I had seen the glasses, book and hat of the missing 'regulars'.

"Thanks, Mr. Waka," says D.I. Moore. "The team can take it from here. Please wait in the car." I walk back to the car alone. I could make a run for it, but I don't. I need to know what happened to Quiet Chinese and Tall Nigerian. Instead, I snooze in the back of the police car.

An hour or so later a black police van pulls up, and a team of divers heads for the pond. The light is beginning to fade by now, but the forensics team erects portable floodlights to continue the search. I get out of the car to stretch my legs. I hear a shout. Through the trees I can see the police gather round something being pulled out of the pond. My curiosity wins, and I stroll over to join them.

A large black canvas travel bag oozing water is being photographed and then opened. Heavy rocks fall out, explaining why the bag has not floated to the surface. From the edge of the small circle of police I see a head emerge from the bag. It looks unscathed and almost peaceful. It is Quiet Chinese.

The rest of his body follows, and it is clearly not unscathed. The chest is open, and I can see the white of his intestines hanging out. I turn to the nearest bush and throw up my breakfast. At this, D.I. Moore notices me, and orders me

47

back to the car. I am pleased to go. I am now sure they will find Tall Nigerian in a similarly gruesome state, and I don't want to be there to see it.

I wait in the car again, and after about twenty minutes D.I. Moore joins me.

"We found the other one. Even worse than the first. I'll spare you the gory details, but they made a mess of his face as well."

"Tall Nigerian," I say, my mind numb. "I knew him as Tall Nigerian." I feel he needs a name, even a fake one.

It is now two months since they pulled the bodies from the pond at Fairlop Waters. I no longer ride the Night Buses. I couldn't return to the N8 even if I had nowhere else to sleep. But I don't need to. I exist again!

My time as an outlaw is over as I have applied for the Leave to Remain in England. I can officially work, and I even have a place to live. OK, it's only a shared room in a run-down tenement in South London, but it sure beats the back seat, top deck of the N8 to Hainault.

I spent several weeks under police protection while they investigated the killings. They uncovered an international organised crime syndicate targeting the homeless and stateless. They found the white van, and inside it a makeshift operating theatre. DNA analysis matched blood in the van to Quiet Chinese and Tall Nigerian among others, and it emerged that the gang was harvesting body parts for sale in the lucrative international black market.

Quiet Chinese kept his eyes due to his myopia, but Tall Nigerian lost his. And I kept my life because a brave bus driver did the right thing. He wasn't going to let something bad happen to one of his passengers, even a homeless bum.

I had swiped my card. I was legal.

Born in Muswell Hill, London, **Chris Dommett** grew up in Essex, attending Campion School in Hornchurch. A degree in French and Russian at St. Andrews University led to a career in banking around the world, including over twenty years in the Middle East.

He is married to Theresa, and they now live in France, beside the beautiful Canal du Midi, with their dog, Marley. When not sampling the local food and wine or playing golf or cricket, Chris enjoys writing fiction, often based loosely on his travels or the characters he has met.

Wickedness in West Norwood

Alice Castle

Beth sat in her kitchen in a state of shock. The unthinkable had happened that bright February morning. Belinda MacKenzie had come up to her outside the gates of Wyatt's and begged for her help.

To say that Belinda was Beth's nemesis was putting it altogether too mildly. For years, the woman had circled Beth like a sumo wrestler preparing to lunge, eyeing up her many weaknesses and waiting to attack.

Beth had never really understood it. She knew she wasn't everyone's cup of tea; she was prickly, short, and definitely opinionated. She thought of herself as shy and retiring but had a feeling that she came across as unfriendly and aloof. She could also be pretty feisty if the situation demanded it. She didn't know why all that got Belinda's back up – but it did.

It wasn't Beth's fault, surely, that so many of Belinda's friends had turned out to be untrustworthy in one way or another during her previous investigations.

But now it seemed Belinda was putting all her many, many reservations behind her. And she was actually asking Beth for her assistance. Well, demanding it might be more accurate.

The first Beth knew of it was when Belinda sidled up to

her. This, in itself, was quite a feat, as Belinda was not much shy of six foot in height, even before pulling on her shiny chestnut boots and her domineering attitude every morning. Beth, meanwhile, would not be knee high to a grasshopper, if there'd been any such creatures in Dulwich. Nevertheless, when Beth heard an urgent "psst" behind her that morning, there she was, crouching down and hissing at her. She really should have guessed it would be Belinda. She'd already got a heady whiff of her nemesis' signature perfume. Beth only hoped it wouldn't give her an instant headache.

"Beth. I need you," Belinda said, her expensive features as close to scrunched up in urgency as they could ever get, thanks to the intervention of her 'darling little botox man' in Lordship Lane. Her piercing blue eyes were the only things that still moved freely, and they widened now in supplication.

Beth was too surprised to perform the obvious manoeuvre and run for the hills as fast as she could. She stayed rooted to the spot, her mouth a little open.

"Let's get a coffee," said Belinda.

These words were always music to Beth's ears, whoever was saying them. And as Katie, Beth's best friend, was busy with a yoga class this morning, it might well be the best offer she was going to get. Curiosity piqued, she trailed off after Belinda, expecting they would go to Belinda's usual café, Jane's, which acted as her unofficial throne room in the Village.

But no. The woman marched down the road, scattering small children and au pairs before her, then beeped open her magnificent 4x4 Land Rover, illegally parked in front of the school's emergency exit. "Get in," she said.

"Am I being kidnapped?" asked Beth, with a nervous giggle.

Belinda sat across from her, swishing her mane of blonde hair, and looked her up and down. She said nothing, merely turning the ignition. With an ominous click, the child lock went on.

Well, that's that. I can't escape now. Might as well enjoy the ride. Beth sank into the cushiest leather seat she'd ever experienced. It was like nestling inside a freshly fluffed-up marshmallow. Belinda's car, with its wall-to-wall pale pink carpets, was a lot plusher than Beth's house. It also had TV screens built into every flat surface and a navigational system that could have put them down on the surface of Mars. Belinda yanked the wheel and pulled out into the traffic. Soon Dulwich, Herne Hill and even Brockwell Park were flashing by.

Where on earth are we going? The question hovered on Beth's lips, but they were travelling at such break-neck speed that she didn't like to risk a crash by breaking Belinda's concentration. Besides, the velocity was pressing her back into her seat and the soft upholstery soon lulled her senses. She was almost sorry when they finally reached their destination. She peered through the window. The car was parked with two wheels up on the pavement, on a double yellow line, right outside a café.

"Here we are," announced Belinda crisply, jumping out and banging the car door shut behind her. Once Beth had finally extracted herself from her squishy cocoon and was on the street too, she could see a new Picturehouse Cinema and a library, a branch of Tesco and lots of little independent shops jostling for attention. It must be, it was… It was West Norwood. She looked at Belinda in surprise. She wouldn't have guessed the woman knew the place existed, let alone popped in for coffees.

"What? Never been to Norwood?" said Belinda, beeping the car to lock it and stalking into the café.

That was how Beth had found herself nose to nose with Belinda over a clandestine cappuccino. It made a sort of sense. If they'd gone to Jane's, Dulwich's premier yummy mummy café, they would have been the cynosure of all eyes. The enmity between Beth and Belinda was as well-known and as bitter as that of Salieri and Mozart, Liam and Noel Gallagher…and possibly even Rebecca Vardy and Colleen Rooney. Here, there were no witnesses to Belinda's strange U-turn.

Belinda immediately started to root around in her fabulously new, unspeakably expensive Mulberry handbag. Beth got tantalising glimpses of the latest iPhone, several must-have lipsticks, a fancy spray of Belinda's beloved Je Reviens perfume and a large pot of La Prairie's Skin Caviar. A bag of delicious-looking biscuits tumbled onto the table. Yum. Almost of its own volition Beth's hand sneaked out towards these, only for Belinda to snap, "They're for the dogs." Trust Belinda's mutts to enjoy treats that looked way better than anything Beth fed herself or her son.

Eventually, Belinda found what she was looking for. She slapped a letter down on the table between them. Beth eyed it cautiously. After the dog biscuits she wasn't taking any chances.

"Well, go on, then." Belinda sighed. "Have a look."

Beth picked the envelope up and slid out a single folded sheet of notepaper. The stationery seemed to be bog standard stuff. But receiving a handwritten letter was unusual in itself these days – who still put pen to paper? Beth got her answer when she read it. A twenty-four-carat weirdo.

Your husband has been playing away. Wouldn't you like to know who with?

Poison pen letters, that's what these were called. She'd heard of them, but never seen one before. She made a few quick observations. Block capitals, very neatly done. Black biro. The sort that was sold in every post office, Rymans and WHSmiths up and down the land. The message itself, though – was this why Belinda had summoned her to coffee? Was it, could it really be true? Was Barney MacKenzie having an affair?

Beth tried to formulate the question in a way which wouldn't have Belinda reaching for her throat across the table. She didn't want her windpipe compromised before she'd had a chance to drink her cappuccino. But, for once, Belinda made things easy for her.

"I don't know if it's true or not. But... I wouldn't put it

past him."

Beth was a little taken aback. Yes, Belinda was terrifying and yes, everyone in Dulwich (and probably within a fifty-mile radius, come to that) took it for granted that Barney, despite owning a magnificent collection of red chinos and cords, definitely did not wear the trousers in his own home. He might well want to assert himself by having the odd fling behind Belinda's back. But would he actually dare to do it? *Would Barney have the balls?* She had to bury her sniggers in her coffee.

"Well?" Belinda was at her most imperious. "Something amusing you?"

"No, no, just wondering… I mean, what exactly do you want me to do about this? Shouldn't you just go to the police? I could show it to Harry if you like…" Much to her own, and everyone else's, astonishment, Beth was still going strong with DI York, the towering Metropolitan Police officer she'd encountered on her first case.

"NO! No," Belinda all but shouted. Once the people at nearby tables had got over their shock and started up their conversations again, she said more quietly, "I want to keep this as confidential as possible, and I don't want to drag the police into it. Anyway, what could they do? They don't arrest people for being unfaithful."

"No, no, I meant they could find out who sent it? That's what you want, isn't it?"

For the second time that day, Belinda surprised Beth. "That's not what I want at all. I don't care who the hell sent it. I just want to know if it's *true*."

Beth sat for a second, fiddling with a sugar sachet. "So you want me to…"

Belinda yanked the sugar out of her hand, exactly as if Beth was one of her three browbeaten children. "That's right, Beth. I want you to do what you do best. Poke your nose into something that isn't your business."

The kitchen clock on the wall seemed to be mocking Beth. Its hands had inched round relentlessly since she'd arrived

55

back from her unexpected audience with Belinda, and it was now almost time for Ben to straggle back from school. And yet she was no further on.

Belinda had slammed off in her car, leaving Beth to find her own way back from West Norwood. It was lucky that today hadn't been one of her allotted sessions in the Archives Office at Wyatt's, as she wouldn't have got a thing done, what with finding the right bus, trudging from the stop to the school – and dealing with her whirring mind.

Some might say that was par for the course with Beth. She was always full of good intentions, planning to curate new and stunning displays of historical material throwing light on the school's glorious past (though not too much, in view of the founder's appalling human rights record). But something usually got in her way. Often it was an actual dead body, so at least Belinda's problem was refreshing. No one seemed to have died. Yet. Beth was a little bit worried that, if she did prove Barney had been unfaithful, his life expectancy might be severely curtailed.

How on earth was she supposed to go about this, anyway? Harry would have found the whole thing so much easier to sort out. With a forensic lab and lots of willing CSIs at his disposal, he would have been able to identify the letter's author in minutes and no doubt wrap up the business by interrogating them in a suitably intimidating police cell.

Beth supposed she could tail Barney. She'd done that before, for a recent case, and although she hadn't been particularly successful (she shushed the voice in her head which added an unhelpful *as usual*) she had at least managed to rule out various lines of enquiry through the endeavour. She'd had assistance from her great friend, Nina, though that wasn't entirely a plus – her car still gave out a heady aroma of spilled Lucozade and trampled Wotsits on wet days. And tailing people took up so much time, time she'd much rather utilise slumped in front of a Scandi Noir box set like the rest of Dulwich.

Could she hack Barney's phone or his email? It didn't take her long to dismiss this idea. Again, the police would have been far better placed to do this. She could only just about manage her own phone most of the time. She supposed she could check Tinder. To her horror, she'd once found another friend's husband lurking on the dating site. But surely Barney wouldn't be that stupid. Would he?

It was intriguing that Belinda wasn't interested in the writer's identity at all. It suggested a level of self-awareness that Beth hadn't realised the woman possessed. Because there was definitely a legion of potential suspects out there, all with compelling motives to attack her. Au pairs, dog walkers, decorators, music teachers, Tai Chi instructors, maths coachers, boiler engineers, even lawyers and accountants. Anyone employed by Belinda, whether for a one-off consultation or a live-in position, was bound to be scarred by the experience. There were enough axes to grind out there to stock a special exhibition at the Tower of London.

Beth sighed. Her last case had involved the death of an estate agent, and she had rapidly discovered that anyone who had moved house in Dulwich in the last decade had a fully-formed motive. She thought back to the first murder she'd stumbled upon, which had involved a limited number of suspects within a constrained time frame. She'd been highly traumatised by the experience then. But now a part of her couldn't help thinking, *ah, those were the days.*

Suddenly Beth realised there was one rich source of information she'd been forgetting – a vein which, if she tapped into it correctly, could probably have told her the secrets of everyone in Dulwich and the rest of south east London too. She pulled out her phone and started pressing buttons, just at the moment when she heard a familiar sound at the door. That was Ben, back already, with homework to be dragged through and a festering gym kit to be decontaminated. She put the phone aside, got up quickly and tried to snap into mother mode. She'd have time to make that call later, when her boy was safely in bed.

But when the clock was finally chiming eleven, Beth was no longer in the kitchen but already tucked up herself. Sometimes she felt that Ben had a lot more stamina than she did. He certainly resisted bedtime in whole new ways, and he was really too old, at twelve, for her to be constantly bursting in and turning off his lights. He could still watch his tablet in the dark anyway. She cursed her feckless older brother, Josh, for the umpteenth time. It was all very well for Ben's childless uncle to lavish expensive gifts on his only nephew, but Beth was the one who had to deal with the consequences. Now, in these days of wall-to-wall porn and gaming, she dreaded to think what Ben, once her innocent little boy, was accessing. Short of cutting off the Wi-Fi in the house (which would have left her and Harry twiddling their thumbs, to be honest) she could only hope for the best.

The next day was bright and crisp again, and Beth wandered to Wyatt's the regulation two steps behind Ben, keeping an anxious eye out for Belinda. She didn't want to have to confess to her lack of progress. She was just slipping through the ornate iron gates, joyfully sure she'd got away with it, when a familiar waft of expensive scent billowed her way. Damn. Then that foghorn voice bellowed out. "Beth! Beth Haldane! A *word,* please."

Beth, cursing under her breath and feeling much more empathy with the note-writer than with its recipient, turned reluctantly and trailed back to Belinda, who was tapping a burnished boot (a different pair, naturally) in impatience.

"I suppose it's too much to ask if you've sorted that little business out?"

Beth was staggered. Belinda surely couldn't be expecting results in twenty-four hours? But even as she reeled in incredulity, she felt the ghosts of a legion of sacked violin teachers at her shoulder, nodding sadly. Yes, she *could* expect results that fast. And she always did, despite the almost total lack of talent demonstrated by her offspring.

"I'm working on it. And, speaking of work…" But if Beth thought that was going to get her out of a confrontation, she hadn't got Belinda's full measure yet.

"One moment. As I'm your employer now…"

Beth stared at her. She'd been so shocked by their

exchange yesterday, and in a way so flattered, against her own will, that Belinda was entrusting such a delicate affair to her, that she hadn't questioned two things. Whether or not she'd take on the assignment, and what she was actually going to get out of it. Maybe now was the moment? They were in public – wherever Belinda went in the confines of the Village, there tended to be a gaggle of less successful, less wealthy wannabe yummies straggling behind her, unprepossessing cygnets to her swan in full sail. There would be witnesses, if things got nasty.

"We haven't really discussed, erm, remuneration…" Beth said, gulping. Mentioning money and confronting Belinda were two cardinal sins which went against every Dulwich grain. She really wasn't sure which was worse.

"Oh, Barney will get you a little job. Didn't I say?"

Beth was open-mouthed. That would be amazing – if it were true. Barney was the head honcho of a massive communications company, as well as on the board of a bank and a man who still had enough fingers free to insert them into any number of corporate pies. Anyone would think he was trying to spend as much time at work as possible, in order to avoid something – or someone. Beth was in dire need of one of his 'little jobs'. Her sinecure at Wyatt's, though she loved it, was not coming anywhere near covering the school fees, despite her staff discount. This could be the godsend she'd been hoping for.

"Erm, OK then," she faltered. "That's great. I'll let you know how I'm getting on, in due course…" She attempted to sidle off again.

"Not so fast. I want a full run-down of your activities so far. Right now," said Belinda, at her most imperious. Beth thought for a moment and realised that saying she'd spent hours yesterday staring into space in her own kitchen was not really going to cut it. She improvised.

"I've put out various feelers. I'm making enquiries and I'm, er, considering some pursuit strategies," she said, drawing herself up to her full height and staring very hard at Belinda's midriff in what she hoped was a no-nonsense sort of way.

Belinda snorted. "Hm, so nothing, then. Well, OK. You've got two days. And then," she paused dramatically before leaning down to Beth's level. "Well, let's just say…you'll see." With that, she turned on her heel and strutted down the road.

Beth stared after her for a moment, before the chiming of the great Wyatt's bell reminded her that she had a job – or jobs – to do.

She had almost got as far as her office door before her terror of Belinda trumped the thought of her towering in-tray. She did an abrupt about-turn and retraced her steps towards Reception. Her great friend Janice currently worked in the back room here, at what some would say was the easiest job in London – head of Wyatt's Pupil Recruitment Strategy. Applicants outnumbered places by at least ten to one. She was also the wife of the school's Head, Dr Grover, and mother of Beth's little goddaughter, Libby.

Beth tapped on the door and popped her head round. Janice, attired in a fluffy cashmere cardigan in a delectable crocus shade that wouldn't have lasted a minute on Beth before getting stained, torn or ravaged by moths, was frowning gently at her screen. She brightened up at the sight of her friend.

"Beth! Take my mind off all this budget nonsense. Tell me all the gossip."

"Oh, but I've come to get it from you. I was just about to ring you yesterday when Ben got back and then I didn't have a chance. You hear everything…"

"Not every single thing," said Janice modestly, though they both knew that was untrue. Every bit of Dulwich news that was fit to print – and a lot that wasn't – flowed past her beautiful shell-like ears. "But what's on your mind?"

"You won't believe it, Belinda's asked me for help…" Beth tailed off, sitting down opposite Janice. She didn't want to be totally indiscreet and start a rumour about Barney if the man was innocent. On the other hand, she really needed to know if Janice had already heard anything on the grapevine.

To her astonishment, Janice promptly slid open her desk drawer. "Do you mean she's had one of these?" she asked, laying out a sheet of notepaper. In block capitals, the message read,

Your husband has been playing away. Wouldn't you like to know who with?

"Oh my God!" said Beth involuntarily. She had spent an unfortunate couple of nights a while ago tailing Janice's husband on far flimsier grounds than this. She shot her friend an extremely worried look.

"Don't panic. This wasn't addressed to me. It was one of the girls in the Junior School who got it. She brought it over. And anyway, I've got past all that rubbish. Tommy wouldn't look at anyone else, I know that really."

That was a huge weight off Beth's mind in itself. She loved Janice and Libby to bits, and she couldn't have borne it if Dr Grover had been doing the dirty. "Do you mind?" asked Beth, gesturing to the note.

Janice obligingly handed it over.

"You didn't consider giving it to the police or anything?" Beth asked.

Janice looked a bit shifty. "Well, for about a second. But the girl didn't want me to. And the police are so over-worked. Poor Harry. The last thing he needs is more nonsense to investigate in Dulwich."

Beth couldn't help but agree. Harry would not be amused to be dragged into another contretemps among the chattering classes while people were being stabbed all along the area's borders. She silently studied the note.

To all intents and purposes, it was identical to Belinda's. The same neat capitals, the same amount of pressure applied to the paper, the same – or a very similar – pen.

"Did you keep the envelope?" Beth asked. Janice shook her head. That was a blow. She tried to still the panic that was now beginning to engulf her.

If this was a full-blown poison pen campaign developing, it wouldn't just be Belinda needing her help. Once again, she

61

was going to find herself seriously out of her depth. If word spread that Belinda had asked for her guidance, and she'd let her down and allowed the letter-writer to target others…well, she'd be ridiculed all around the Village.

She knew it was silly even to worry about such things. She had never been popular, so she didn't have much to lose. But there was a difference between choosing to avoid people like Belinda – and simply being shunned by the whole of Dulwich. Plus, she'd be branded a total failure at her strange little side-line of investigating mysteries – and that did matter.

She felt a clutch of irrational dread. No, she had to remain calm, she told herself.

Don't get this out of proportion. Do like Katie always tells you. Take a few deep breaths, regain a sense of calm.

As she puffed in and out, under Janice's slightly amused gaze, the thin paper in her hand fluttered.

Beth blinked a couple of times and then sat up a little straighter. And put her head on one side, as enlightenment dawned.

If she wasn't mistaken, she'd just had a total brainwave.

She held the paper right up to her face and studied it as though her life depended on it. At this stage, she felt as if it did.

Janice, on the other side of the desk, laughed. "Are you trying to memorise the message? It's only one line. Shouldn't be that difficult."

"No… It's just, oh, Janice, thank you so much, but I need to rush off. Is it OK if I take this?" Beth asked, waving the paper. "Oh, and do you have a plastic bag I could put it in?"

Janice glided towards her stationery cupboard and fished out a little sachet that was just the right size. Beth slid the note carefully inside it as her friend looked on, bemused. "Isn't it a bit late for all that 'preserving the evidence' malarkey? I mean, we've both got our prints all over it, not to mention the girl who received it in the first place…"

Beth smiled enigmatically and brushed her fringe out of the way with her free hand. Inexorably, it swung back but her grin stayed in place. "Just had a bit of an idea. Keep your fingers crossed for me," she said as she dashed out of the office.

As the door closed, Beth could have sworn she heard Janice saying quietly, "I always do."

Beth was toying with the spoon in her cappuccino saucer when someone sat down heavily opposite her in Jane's.

"This had better be good. I was about to walk my dogs when I got your garbled message. Their poor little faces," Belinda MacKenzie said, flicking her elaborately streaky blonde hair over her shoulder. She threw her bag onto the table, sloshing Beth's coffee everywhere.

As Beth knew from Katie, Belinda's neighbour, that her dogs were in fact towed round the Park every day by a team of walkers, she decided not to feel a moment's guilt. Instead she wondered, for the umpteenth time, how Belinda got her mane so poker-straight. She put a hand up to her own collapsing ponytail, then shrugged. She had more important things to deal with.

"You asked me to look into a letter you received about, er, Barney," she said.

"Yes. And while you've been getting nowhere, several of my friends have had them as well," said Belinda, shaking her head angrily.

Beth breathed in and started to look a bit more confident.

"Were they identical?" she asked.

"Well, actually they were. What's that got to do with anything? As you know, what I asked you to find out was not who sent the note, but whether what it said was true."

Beth looked at the woman hard and said nothing. Nothing at all. A little puddle of silence developed between them and seemed to stretch from one side of the table to the other. Belinda was now, under Beth's gaze, beginning to turn an interesting shade of pink.

"You seem a little defensive, Belinda. I wonder why that might be?"

"What are you on about, Beth? I don't have time for this. I

have to go. Barney's got clients coming for dinner…"

Belinda made to get up, but Beth spoke quickly. "I think you'll want to stay and hear this, Belinda." As it was well known that Belinda hadn't cooked a meal since posh frozen food company Frost had opened up in the Village, Beth wasn't buying her excuse for disappearing any more than her dog walking gambit.

Belinda subsided, drumming her fingers on the table top. "All right, then. Get on with it."

"At first I was just worried about doing your bidding. Finding out what Barney might be up to, and with whom," Beth said. "Then I realised, unless I followed him twenty-four hours a day, which would involve me going to work with him, or unless I talked to all his friends – and the poor man doesn't really seem to have many – I would never be sure. Then I started wondering why you wanted me to tackle things that way. Getting to the culprit seemed much more logical. But you were so sure you didn't want that."

"And I still am!" Belinda spluttered.

"Yes…but why?" asked Beth. "Why would that be? And then, when I was studying one of the other notes, received by someone at Wyatt's…"

Belinda leaned forward – and Beth got what she'd been waiting for.

"You see," she said slowly. "There it is again."

"There *what* is? Honestly, Beth. I might have known this would happen. You pretend you're a proper private eye, Dulwich's answer to Miss Marple or some nonsense, but you couldn't investigate your way out of a paper bag. I've given you every single chance, offered you a job, even, but no, you're just useless…" Belinda snarled. Now, despite her perfect hairdo, immaculate make-up and carefully curated face, she looked very ugly indeed.

"On the contrary, Belinda. I think you'll find I've solved this case satisfactorily. Despite you giving me next to nothing to go on, and no time to sort things out properly either, I've been able to deduce that there's one person, and one person only, in the whole of Dulwich, who knows whether Barney is being unfaithful or not…"

Beth's voice was now ringing out loud and clear in the café, and for once she didn't mind that all eyes had turned to study their table. Belinda, on the other hand, seemed to be trying to disappear behind her huge handbag.

"And that is…*you*."

There was a loud intake of breath from several clutches of mummies at neighbouring tables. Then, as Belinda turned on them with a basilisk glare, they all became very interested in their pastries, or even their offspring, instead.

"You see, Belinda, there are two obvious questions about a poison pen letter: who wrote it, and whether or not its nasty little message is true. It made no sense at all that you were only interested in half the equation. Then, of course, you gave yourself away completely."

Belinda leaned forward again and hissed at Beth. "I don't know what on earth you mean! How, how *dare* you speak to me this way?"

Beth swayed back in her own seat. "There you go again, you don't even realise what you're doing, how much you're giving yourself away. Even if you didn't write your own name at the bottom, you still added your signature to those letters."

"I bloody didn't! I was so careful…" Belinda started – then stopped abruptly.

"There you are," said Beth, her head on one side. "You've admitted it now. But something else told me it was you anyway. Your perfume."

"My perfume?" Belinda screwed up her face, rooted in her bag, and threw the phial of Je Reviens onto the table. "I'm not the only person who wears this, you know."

"No. But you're the only person who wears *so much*," said Beth, her smile peeping out. "I've explained the whole situation to Janice. She'll be making sure that everyone who got a letter knows the truth. Everyone who hasn't already just overheard the news in here, anyway."

Belinda drew herself up to her full height, gave Beth one last withering look, and stormed out of the café, knocking over a toddler as she did so. In the ensuing cacophony of wailing and twittering from the mummies, agog at developments, Beth was able to slink away almost unnoticed. She had quite a spring in her step as she walked towards her little house in Pickwick Road.

Until she thought things through. That scent, Je Reviens. As well as being pretty pungent, enough to linger on paper days after leaving Belinda's house, its name also contained a promise – or a threat. Wasn't that what the Terminator used to say, at the end of his films? '*I'll be back.*'

Oh dear. Belinda had been her frenemy before. Now it would be more like all-out war in Dulwich. Perhaps it was time Beth got a signature scent of her own. Ma Griffe, by Carven, perhaps? A claw might be handy against an enraged Belinda. Or how about Cartier's Panthère?

As she walked down her garden path, she saw her black and white moggy, Magpie, in the window. The cat seemed to wink at her with one emerald green eye. She smiled again. She didn't need gusts of migraine-inducing perfume to help her, when she had Magpie on her side, not to mention Colin her ancient Labrador, her son Ben, and even the Metropolitan Police, in the comforting shape of Harry. Plus that little old thing called justice, of course.

Long may that, and the Dulwich way of life, prevail, thought Beth, closing her front door behind her.

Before turning to crime, **Alice Castle** was a UK newspaper journalist for The Daily Express, The Times and The Daily Telegraph. Her first book, Hot Chocolate, was a European hit and sold out in two weeks.

Death in Dulwich was published in September 2017 and has been a number one best-seller in the UK, US, Canada, France, Spain and Germany. A sequel, The Girl in the Gallery, was published in December 2017 to critical acclaim and also hit the number one spot. Calamity in Camberwell, the third book in the London Murder Mystery series, was published in August 2018, with Homicide in Herne Hill following in October 2018. Revenge on the Rye came out in December 2018. The Body in Belair Park was released in June 2019, and The Slayings in Sydenham followed in December 2019.

Alice is currently working on the eighth London Murder Mystery adventure. It will feature Beth Haldane and DI Harry York again.

Alice also writes psychological thrillers for HQDigital under the name A. M. Castle.

Check her websites **www.alicecasteauthor.com** and **www.dulwichdivorcee.com** for news on all her publications.

A Tale from the Ball's Pond Road

Richard Savin

Running into Harry at Waterloo station that day was a surprise. I had forgotten about him and deep in my sub-conscious probably supposed him to be dead; but there he was, walking across the concourse at Waterloo, frail but still upright. He must have been in his eighties.

I first met Harry when I worked for him, picking up the pots and occasionally serving behind the bar in his pub. The job was an unofficial, part time arrangement, and I was paid under the counter, so to speak. You see, I was still a student and only sixteen, which was too young to work in licensed premises; though nobody seemed much bothered in those days. Harry owned the Green Man in North London, just off the Balls Pond Road, around the corner from the button factory. That was in 1955, and it would be thirty years before I saw him again.

It was a fine Saturday morning in spring. In the narrow cul-de-sac known as Haliday Walk, Charlie Wooten and Big Bill stood outside The Green Man. They leaned casually against the cream tiled wall of the pub, dragging on their fags and looking admiringly at Bill's new Lee Enfield Silver Bullet. Charlie was five foot two, Big Bill was six three, and they were locally known as Shorty and Lofty. They had become friends when they were nippers at junior school, and Big Bill had saved Charlie from a beating by One Eye Bevin the school bully. The fight, in which Bevin had come off worse, had immediately created a life-long friendship between them; but it had also raised a festering rancour between Bill and One Eye, and they had never spoken a civil word to each other since.

One Eye Bevin actually had two eyes, but one of them had a cast and looked away to the left and it was as useful as if he had not got it at all; and so that is how he was known.

If Big Bill was tall, then Bevin was wide. He had been stocky as a boy and had grown into a solid hulk as he moved into his adolescence. He had a nasty streak in him too. He delighted in the torture of those weaker than him and once, when they had gone into the countryside of Essex on a school outing, he had occupied himself in searching the hedgerows for the nests of finches, and slitting the throats of the fledgling birds with a razor blade. He grew ugly into his teens, and bigger – and nastier. At eighteen, he had roamed the streets with a bunch of unpleasant youths known locally as the Pepperface Gang; always on the lookout for a victim and a chance to inflict humiliation. Ultimately, as many had predicted, he had ended up doing time: six months in Pentonville Prison for ABH. Inside the walls of that Victorian institution he developed a reputation as a man best avoided. Everyone trod carefully around him for fear of the vicious retribution he meted out to those who stepped on the wrong side of him. He was a man whose acquaintance was not sought out; even the screws gave him a wide berth and if they did have to attend upon him, they always went two-handed.

In the saloon bar on that day, the lunch time drinkers had already settled in. Brown Ale Bert, with a big gold and diamond ring on his right hand, was casually engaged in a conversation with a detective sergeant up from the Snow Hill station. DS Gittens was on the take, and he'd come to Bert for his monthly payoff. It was a common arrangement in those times; every villain had their patch, and every patch had a copper on the make. Like a witch's familiar, they worked the magic that kept the underworld in order. A little bit of oil on the wheels so that nothing or nobody squeaked.

Bert pulled up the sleeve of his camel hair overcoat to reveal a forearm clamped around with six Swiss watches. He was not a fence, you understand; he operated a second-hand car lot just along St. Paul's Road. But his brother was in the army, stationed in Germany – and all manner of tradable contraband came Bert's way.

He slipped a flashy Omega, with a gilt bracelet, off his wrist and dropped it into the pocket of Gittens' overcoat. They talked for a while in low tones then the detective sergeant took his leave. He would not be back for another month, and Bert could rest certain that no other policeman would come feeling his collar.

At the end of the bar closest to the door, Diamond Mini sat perched on a stool, a large gin and tonic in one hand, a fur wrap around her shoulders and a cigarette held delicately between her fingers. It was rumoured her jewellery, of which she had plenty, had previously been the property of an Italian countess and that it had been liberated by sleight of hand at the end of the war. No questions were asked but, word had it, it was worth more than the house in which she lived, together with her Italian husband, Giorgio.

Down at the far end of the bar, Fat Sophie, the local call girl, sat perched on her regular bar stool, waiting for whatever might come her way. She always ordered the same drink, gin with a splash of Fernet Branca and a dash of Angostura Bitters. Her eyes were dark, her lipstick bright red, and she wrapped herself in a beaver lamb fur coat like a package waiting to be opened. To me, as a sixteen-year-old, she carried the air of some exotic, eastern concubine; voluptuous, mysterious, and unattainable.

"Stop leerin'!" Mini let out a shrill cackle and swiped the back of her hand across Giorgio's shoulder with a thump. "You ain't gettin' your cock into that."

Harry, the landlord, wagged a finger at her and told her to

behave, whereupon she went off into paroxysms of raucous laughing.

It could have been any Saturday at the Green Man, in the early spring of 1955, except that later on that night there would be trouble. Not that trouble was a stranger to the Green Man. Built in 1898 on a small plot at the end of Haliday Walk, it had seen plenty of action. The Walk was no more than a narrow alley. It let onto St. Paul's Road, a short step from the crossroads; turn left and you were heading for Dalston Junction where there was a street market every Saturday. It was a place where you could buy just about anything – so long as you were not too fussy about its provenance.

If you turned right into Essex Road then you were heading for The Angel of Islington. Just on the Green there was Collins Music Hall, a Victorian institution of entertainment that staged shows with lightly clad girls and off-colour jokes. It had a reputation not unlike that of Dalston Market.

It is fair to say that these were environments in which the occasional fracas would likely take place.

The Green Man had three bars, of which the saloon bar was the largest. It had elegant etched mirrors, chandeliers and a stout covering of brown lino on the floor, which was kept polished to a high sheen. It was ships' lino, originally destined for the officer's quarters on a destroyer, but had somehow been diverted. It had been acquired on behalf of Harry by Brown Ale Bert, from a man in the market, down at Dalston Junction. No questions were asked, and no answers given. Some cash and a barrel of mild ale changed hands and the lino was laid by a local, Irish Tom, whose real job was being a chauffeur.

Then there was the snug. A small private space with benches and a welcoming open fire, usually the haunt of the old men and women who liked to keep their drinking to themselves.

Finally, there was the public bar: no frills, and a darts

board hung on the wall at one end next to the toilets. It had a wood planked floor that was covered in a fresh layer of sawdust every evening so that those who wanted to, could spit or slop their ale as the fancy took them. It was in the public bar that there was most likely to be some excitement.

Charlie Wotton rubbed at the chain grease on his hands with a rag. "There's gonna be a punch-up," he pronounced with an air of one who is sure of his facts, then stuffed the grubby cloth into his pocket. "That Dodgy Dave Watson, 'ee's been puttin' it about wiv some slut down at the Elephant and Castle. I 'erd they was coming up 'ere mob-'anded tonight."

Big Bill shrugged his lanky frame and jerked his head towards the door of the public bar. "Come on, let's get a drink."

In the saloon bar, his arrangements complete, Bert lit up a small cheroot, flashed a smile at Diamond Mini, downed the dregs of his brown ale and left, doffing his trilby hat as he took his leave.

In that same moment I was also leaving the bar, clumping along with my leg in a plaster cast, on account of having broken two toes in the school gym the week before.

"I'm going to Dalston market," I shouted to Harry. "Anything you want?"

"Yes." He leaned across the bar counter. "You know the music shop in Balls Pond Road? Drop in and ask the piano tuner to come up here. Lou's playing on it tonight and he's complaining top G is flat."

Frankly, I was not surprised, given the amount of beer that had found its way into the works over the years.

Lou the piano player was a small wiry man in a shiny blue suit. Birth had not been kind to him; he had a deformed shoulder which made him sit hunched at the piano. His complexion was sallow and, when he smiled, he displayed an uneven jumble of badly placed teeth, one of which was gold. Though the gold tooth did him no favours; its perfect profile stood up like a tombstone in a graveyard and simply served

73

to underline how awful the rest of its disorderly companions were.

But for all of his misfortunes of birth, Lou Kaufman had one blessing: he was a gifted pianist. It was commonly reported that he had once played with a great concert orchestra – in Vienna, some said, though nobody seemed to know why he was now reduced to playing in Collins Music Hall; or why he played for a few shillings on a Saturday night in the saloon bar of the Green Man – with no better instrument to play on than a badly tuned rosewood upright. There *was* speculation, but nobody knew. Not that it mattered to him. He was a friendly soul and on a Saturday night he would sit at the battered upright and play pretty much anything requested.

Lou had a small dog that accompanied him everywhere; a scruffy brown mongrel with a broken tail. It answered to the name of Ridley. The dog would sit quietly under the lee of the piano keyboard where it watched with suspicion the passage of legs that paraded past its gaze.

At four o'clock the piano tuner arrived with a small felt hammer and a tuning key. When he lifted the lid, he shook his head in disapproval at the condition of the instrument; but no matter, one by one he tensioned the wires turning the tuning pins with the key and tapping each wire with his felt hammer.

"You've got one in there that's near to breaking," the tuner eventually announced to Harry. "It won't last much longer. I'll take it out and replace it; they're not cheap, you know."

When he had finished, he packed away his tools and with the air of a man who knows his entitlements, went to the bar for one on the house. "Here." He waved the worn-out wire, which he had neatly coiled, and offered it to Harry. "You might as well throw this in the bin."

Big Bill, always on the lookout for something for nothing, intercepted the prize with an outstretched hand. "That's a useful bit of wire, that is. Don't bin it, I'll 'ave it."

Charlie Wotton expressed his approval with a knowing

nod. "Can always find a use for a good bit of wire."

The tuner finished his complimentary drink and took his leave, firing a parting shot as he went. "And don't pour anymore beer into that piano or those wires won't last – they'll just go rusty."

At seven o'clock the first signs of the trouble to come turned up as a small mob of strangers walked into the public bar. They ordered drinks and stood there sullenly looking around at the other customers. Charlie nudged Big Bill who was about to throw his final dart for a double 16 finish.

Big Bill paused and looked over his shoulder. "They look a bit tasty," he hissed under his breath. "You seen Dodgy?"

Charlie nodded in the direction of the saloon bar.

Bill wagged his head from side to side in a gesture of disapproval. "I warned 'im not to come, silly boy." With that he threw the dart and planted it neatly between the outer wires of the number 16 on the board. "Game, I think. Your turn to buy."

Going to the bar to get the round and looking across the counter, Charlie could see directly into the saloon, where he found himself staring at the face of Dodgy Dave Watson.

On the tables, the empty glasses were piling up as the sound of the piano rose into the air, punctuated by the ring of the cash register and the squirting of the beer pumps; and all mingled with the cacophony of voices as the regulars slowly drifted in. A blue haze of tobacco smoke began to fill the air.

Brown Ale Bert had taken up his usual position, casually reposed with one elbow on the bar. He took a cigarette out of a pig-skin leather case and, with a deft flick of a solid gold Dunhill lighter, lit up. He snapped the Dunhill shut, drew hard on the cigarette and blew out a long stream of blue smoke.

Next to him Dodgy Dave had sidled up to the bar, one arm around his latest conquest: the girl from the Elephant and Castle. Her hair was very blonde and her makeup heavily applied. She wore a pale blue cardigan top that stretched tight across a pointy brassiere, a broad black patent leather belt and a wide floral skirt that billowed out over the support of three sugar nylon petticoats. She stood there perched on four-inch heels that looked like they might snap at any moment.

Dave turned and grinned. "Bert, I'd like you to meet Yvonne."

The girl shimmied closer, put out a hand and giggled. "Nice to meet you, Bert."

In the public bar, Eric, who was now everybody's friend on account of having had a big win on the football pools, ordered a glass of Worthington's IPA. He was offering drinks to Big Bill and Charlie when the door opened, and One Eye Bevin came in. Now, though it was not strictly his local because One Eye had moved to a place close to Southwark Bridge and often crossed the river to drink, he occasionally came into the Green Man – it was said, just to annoy Big Bill.

The assembled company of the public bar turned to look as One Eye joined the group of strangers who were by then looking across the counter and through to the saloon where Dodgy Dave could be seen with an arm around Yvonne. The group conferred, then downed their drinks and made their way to the toilets, which were communal and connected both bars.

From the snug, three elderly ladies gave the men a worried glance. "Elephant and Castle boys," one of them whispered under her breath, "that'll be aggravation, you just mark my words."

Charlie and Big Bill watched as the mob trooped in single file towards the toilet.

"Someone needs to warn Dave," Charlie said quietly. "Come on, let's go round the other way."

They left through the street exit of the public bar, walked to the saloon bar and pushed open the door.

At the piano, Lou had struck up the Londonderry Air, and Irish Tom was in full voice, his pint of stout standing on the lid.

Of course, I remember that night very well; I was serving Fat Sophie her usual gin and Fernet, when Harry called out that the tables were getting a bit loaded and I should go around and collect the empty glasses and bottles. I lifted the flap and, after persuading Diamond Mini and Giorgio to shift along a bit, I clumped in my plaster cast out into the crowd.

Irish Tom, having murdered the Londonderry Air, was trying to persuade Lou to play Irish Eyes.

Under the cover of the keyboard, Ridley the dog sat patiently, staring out through his small brown eyes at the chaos of legs and voices that filled his world.

I had just deposited two handfuls of pint glasses on the counter when the mob from the public bar emerged from the toilets.

Seeing the Elephant mob coming their way, Charlie shouted out over the heads of the crowd. "Oi, Dave, over 'ere."

Dave stood there looking bewildered and shaking his head, a stupid grin on his face. Charlie shouted some more and Big Bill, who stood a head taller than the rest of the customers, gesticulated frantically. Dave finally got the message and giving Yvonne a peck on the cheek, he squeezed a handful of her left buttock and started towards them. He got no more than a step or two when the first of the Elephant mob stepped into his way.

"Where you goin', Dalston scum?" the man snarled and hit Dave with the heel of his hand hard in the shoulder, pushing him back. "Not so fast, mate." He hit him again, this time in the chest, driving Dave up against the bar.

Yvonne screamed and stepped between her man and his assailant, a lad with whom she was familiar. "What the fuck d'ya think you're up to, Tone?"

Another of the mob pulled on her shoulder yelling, "Shut up, you dirty slag. What the fuck're you doin' 'ere with these shitbags?"

Then another joined in. "You oughta stay where you belong, Yvonne; you're the wrong side of the fucking river, my girl."

In the same instance Dave waded in, yelling for them to "fuck off back to the Elephant."

Voices were now angry and raw; the regulars started to step away. A fourth, much younger member of the mob, a pasty looking teenager with a pimply face and dark greasy hair joined in, repeatedly prodding Dave in the chest. Dave flung a wild punch at the youth hitting him squarely on the nose. The youth let out a howl and staggered back.

Diamond Mini got down off her stool and laid into the nearest one, yelling a string of expletives in her shrill voice. She placed herself firmly between Yvonne and the assailants. "That's enough, lads. Now cut it out."

Giorgio piled in to support her, going at them like a terrier. "Calm down, lads, you heard what the lady said. Just leave it out. We don't want the police coming around."

For a moment the chaos abated, and it looked as if Mini had shocked some sense into them.

Yvonne was sobbing.

Then one of the mob pulled out a cut-throat razor that he carried tucked up behind his ear, under his cap. He flicked the blade across her face and in the same moment spat on her, yelling, "That'll give you something to remember us by, slut."

She let out a whimper and put her hand to the slash wound. A fine red line began to weep tears of blood.

The man with the razor leered at her.

In the same space of time, the other three laid into Dave, and he fell to the floor. Some of the men in the bar joined in to help Dave. Fists began to fly. Women ran screaming out into the street as the fight degenerated into an all-out brawl. By the time Big Bill reached him, Dave was in a mess. He had been kicked and pummelled senseless. Between them, Bill and several other customers managed to pull the mob away. They marched them to the exit and bundled them out into the street. Bill stood guard at the door for a while, but the Elephant and Castle mob had decided to call it a day.

Dave was in a bad way, but Harry was adamant they should not call the police or an ambulance. A fight like that was enough to get his licence suspended if it got to the ears of the local magistrate. Instead they took Dave to an upstairs room and Bert called a doctor he knew who was familiar with this kind of problem and could be relied upon to keep his mouth shut.

Down in the saloon bar, Bill had come back in and was sipping on a pint thoughtfully provided by Eric who had watched the fracas from the safety of the public bar. Over at the piano, Lou had started on a Frank Sinatra number and Ridley had settled back down under the keyboard.

One Eye Bevin, who had been with the Elephant mob but who had not joined in the fight, went over to the piano and leaned on one corner, glaring over at Bill.

Lou stopped playing. "Would you mind not leaning on it," he asked politely. "It interferes with the tone."

One Eye looked down at the small man in the shiny blue suit. He put out a ham fist and took hold of Lou's delicate fingers, then squeezed. Lou winced. One Eye squeezed harder.

"'Ow would you like me to break yer fingers, ya little git?" He let go and leaned back on the piano.

"Why don't you leave him alone?" a man sitting at a table close to the piano protested. "He isn't doing you any harm."

That was enough for One Eye who swiftly went across and punched the punter, knocking him off his chair.

"Oh God," a woman screamed.

Lou was a mild-mannered man, but this was too much. "There was no call for that," he snapped.

One Eye sneered at him then, spotting Ridley, he grabbed the dog by its tail, swung it round a couple of times then threw it the length of the saloon bar where it bounced off the wall. Ridley fell broken to the floor. One Eye lifted the piano lid and reaching in, physically ripped out the first two strings that came into his grasp.

"Now see how that interferes with the tone."

It took Bill less than the count of three to reach One Eye and land a solid punch to the side of his head. It failed to knock him down, but he staggered and clutched at the piano for support. Pulling himself upright, he picked up a pint glass from the nearest table and threw the contents into Bill's face, smashed the glass on the table and shoved the broken edge hard into Bill's cheek. Bill roared. Grabbing One Eye, he pummelled him with blows to the head and chest.

One Eye broke free and picking up a chair, smashed it down onto Bill's shoulders. Big Bill dropped in a heap, unconscious. One Eye stood over him for a moment then threw the chair aside, grunted at the onlookers, and walked out into the street. Above the murmur that ensued, the plaintiff sobs of Lou could be heard as he knelt beside Ridley. His little brown-eyed dog was dead.

It was a week since the fight, and nobody had seen Big Bill. Charlie Wotton hung around outside the public bar, polishing his BSA Gold Star, hoping that Bill would turn up on the Silver Bullet, but the wait was in vain. He struck a forlorn figure, dispirited and still trying to come to terms with what had happened. Harry came out from time to time, bringing him a pint but it didn't seem to help. Evil had somehow triumphed over good, and Charlie felt bitter.

In the saloon bar, the talk was all about what had happened and how Dodgy was really to blame for bringing that Elephant girl across the river. "He should ov stayed dahn there," Eric told anyone who would listen and then called Harry to say he was buying the whole pub a round on account of "they needed to *co-rissermate*."

The piano tuner came back and replaced the two strings that One Eye had ripped out, but Lou never returned to play, and the piano stood silent like a memorial stone in a churchyard; a sombre epitaph to unspoken grief.

In the end, Charlie gave up the vigil and he too disappeared. "I'll swing for that bastard One Eye, Harry," he said bitterly as he got astride the Gold Star and kicked the engine into life. "On my baby's life, Harry, I swear I'll kill 'im."

On Sunday, as was the law then, the pub opened from midday till two and then closed; it would be shut till Monday.

"We should go up West," Harry suggested to a few of the regulars, "do a show and have some grub; cheer us all up – it'll do us some good."

Irish Tom, who was the chauffeur to the board of a substantial City firm, drove us in his bosses' Humber limousine: Harry and me with Giorgio and Mini, in the back, while Iris, Tom's wife, sat up front. We must have looked like royalty, what with Mini bundled up in her furs and jewels and the car being so posh; though when I mentioned it they all fell about laughing.

"She looks more like a bloody Christmas tree than royalty," Tom guffawed, gesturing to Mini. Iris elbowed him sharply in the ribs and told him to mind his manners.

We went to the Palladium where Frankie Lane, the American crooner, was showing and afterwards we walked down Piccadilly to the Chicken Inn and ate platefuls of roasted chicken with chips. On the way back to the pub, the talk turned solemnly to Big Bill and Charlie Wotton's absence, and speculation of where they might be.

"It must have been 'ard for Bill," Mini said morosely. "Poor bugger must 'ave taken it bad."

Back at the Green Man, Harry opened up the bar for an illicit party. You had to be careful because from time to time a bobby on the beat might spot the lights, and if he wasn't a local then it could end with a stand-up performance in front of the magistrates.

So, when, with the bar lights dimmed, and a round of drinks on the counter, there was a banging on the door, Harry thought the game was up.

"Toilets," he said, in hardly more than a whisper.

"Men's urinals," Mini sniggered.

Drinks were scooped up and the company moved quickly to hide in the lavatories.

The rapping on the door became more insistent.

"Answer the door," Harry instructed, "and tell them we're cleaning the beer engines."

I made a lot of noise drawing the bolts and turning the key, hoping to convince whoever was waiting on the other side that the pub was well and truly shut. Cautiously, I pulled the door ajar. It was not the police – it was Eric.

"Is Harry there? I need to come in."

Now with all that money Eric had won on the pools, and him being such a free spender, it was hard to refuse – but I thought it best to try. "We're closed, Eric," I said apologetically. "I can't serve you a drink, I'm afraid."

Eric shook his head in short rapid movements. "No, no, no," he protested. "I need to see Harry. I need to tell him something. One Eye Bevin, 'ees copped it – 'ees dead, bin done in."

"Come in," I said, staggering under the weight of the news.

Harry summoned everyone from the toilets and when they were assembled and glasses had been refilled, Eric told what he knew.

"The rozzers were round our street." Eric's voice was low and sombre. "They said they was investigating a murder. Bevin Arnold they said – that's One Eye's name – 'ees been murdered. Strangled apparently, and they were looking for Big Bill."

The discussion went on long and late and glasses were refilled until eventually there was nothing more on which to speculate and everyone drifted off home.

For a whole fortnight the Green Man was packed.

"Crime tourists," Mini complained. "Voyeurs come to see the scene of the crime. Can't get a seat because of them."

Harry wasn't unhappy; business was brisk.

The Dalston Gazette sent a reporter and a photographer, and I got to show off the blood stains that were still on my plaster cast. Later, the Evening Standard carried the story although it was buried away in the middle. The police came and went, asked questions and took statements. Everyone wanted to have a say, it was their moment of celebrity – all except Brown Ale Bert who kept a low profile and arranged his monthly meeting with DS Gittens around the corner in the Mildmay Tavern where he had taken his custom for the time being.

As things settled down Bert returned with a snippet of news. One Eye had been savagely garrotted, DS Gittens had told him. Whoever did it must have been incredibly strong because it had nearly severed the head from the body. The theory was that he had been strangled with a cheese wire.

A few days later, there was the sound of a motorbike in Haliday Walk. Charlie Wotton put the Gold Star on its stand and went into the public bar. I was busy getting a pin of barley wine up onto its chocks and was about to bang in the tap with a bung starter when Charlie walked in. His face looked grave and his eyes dull. I smiled and said, "Watcha," but he looked straight through me.

"It's Bill," he said directly to Harry, "'ees been arrested for murder. Gimme a pint of my usual." He took his pint and without a further word went off into the snug. It was the only time I ever saw Charlie use the snug.

The news was all over the nationals, with a picture of Big Bill right up front. You could see the scars where One Eye had pushed the broken glass into his face.

"Do you suppose he'll hang," I asked Harry.

He screwed up his face and tightened his lips. "Probably," he said, in a voice that was all matter of fact. "Can't see him getting off. They say it was that piano wire he got from the tuner when he came round to fix it. That's what he used to strangle One Eye."

At the end of the summer I said my farewells to Harry and the regulars and left the Green Man. I was due to take my GCE exams the following spring and needed to study, so I went to stay with my sister in Surrey, far away from the distractions of London life.

I never saw Charlie Wotton again, or Diamond Mini,

Giorgio, Brown Ale Bert and the others. I did read one thing though. A month after Big Bill had been handed the death sentence at the Old Bailey there was a stay of execution – a reprieve on the grounds of new evidence that threw doubt over the conviction. But that was it, and slowly they faded from my memory.

I finished my exams and went on to do a further year in the sixth form. In 1958 I joined a firm in the City and settled down to the life of a commuter…

And that is where my story should end – except that on a day in 1999, on the eve of the third millennium, I chanced to run across Harry on the concourse of Waterloo station.

At first, he didn't recognise me, but as it sank in who I was he smiled warmly and suggested we have a drink, for old times' sake. We went into one of the new bars that had opened and I offered to buy the round. We got to talking of the Green Man and the characters who had been its regulars.

"They pulled it down," Harry said, wistfully. "Built a lot of modern houses on the site. The Walk has changed. You wouldn't recognise it."

And that is when we got onto the subject of Big Bill and the murder of One Eye Bevin.

"What was that thing about Big Bill and the murder? He didn't swing, I seem to remember."

"Ah," Harry grinned. "That *was* a surprise."

"So?"

"There was a late confession. You see, as it turned out, it wasn't Bill after all."

"I don't remember reading anything about it. What happened?"

Harry gave a little shrug, raised his eyebrows and tilted his head. "It was all hushed up –a big embarrassment to the Murder Squad at the Yard. They firmly put a lid on it. That's how things were back then. I only heard on the QT from Brown Ale Bert; his protection told him – that bent DS he used to pay off every month."

"So, if not Big Bill, then who?"

Harry chuckled. "You'd never guess in a month of Sundays. Go on, who do you think?"

"I've no idea," I protested. "Not little Charlie Wotton, surely. Mind you, he said he would do for One Eye, as I remember."

"No, not Charlie. I heard he died a few years back. Heart attack."

"OK, so who?"

A beaming smile spread across Harry's face. "It turns out that our killer was in the commandos during the war. By all accounts he was decorated for bravery. Parachuted behind enemy lines no less than seven times. It seems his specialism was garrotting Germans."

"That tells me nothing."

"Here's a bit more of a clue. Later that year, he did a bunk. He turned up in Israel and distinguished himself in the Suez War. It was from there he wrote and sent a confession. There was no chance of getting him back. The Israelis wouldn't put up with sending a hero back here to be hung."

"My God, it was Lou, the piano player?"

"Little Lou in the shiny blue suit."

"Bloody hell! Who'd have guessed."

Harry shook his head slowly. "It was that little brown mongrel of his; that's what did it. One Eye couldn't have known at the time, but when he flung that mutt the length of the saloon bar, he was writing his own death warrant."

We parted with the promise to meet up again some time, though we never did. Slowly, the ghosts of Big Bill, Charlie, Mini and the others faded away. I did go back to look at where the pub had once been, but Harry was right; I didn't recognise the area. The houses were neat, gentrified and pricey, and there was no trace left of what had been.

It had all gone, dissolved into the local folklore, and it would eventually be forgotten.

A lifetime journalist and one time chef/owner of three London restaurants, **Richard Savin**'s first book was published by Canongate in 1979. Vakilabad – Iran, was an account of his experiences during the run up to the Islamic Revolution. In the 1990s he was a regular guest broadcaster with BBC Radio South current affairs. Since then he has gone on to write five novels and is currently working on a sixth.

He has a passion for cooking, wine, classic cars, motorcycling, and travel.

Finding Victoria

Alan Taylor

She is laid out on a simple wooden cross, two painted crossbeams; one black, one blue. A weak ribbon of daylight, stolen from the gap between the thick orange curtains, cuts across her body. She is bound to the cross at her waist, her wrists and her ankles by something that appears to be thick rope, knotted badly. Her flowing white nightdress hangs down to the floor and trails in a puddle of her blood.

The doorbell rings, and she jolts. Her eyes snap open. She is weak, and everything hurts. She struggles but can't move. She turns her head to the side, sees her bound wrist, remembers where she is, what she has done.

She screams, but no noise comes. As she opens her mouth, her tongue becomes a rose, opening and unfurling as though it were dawn.

I will admit that I was somewhat surprised to find myself standing in the dingy corridor of the office block on the corner of Tottenham Court Road and Euston Road. It was early evening on a Friday in the glorious June of 1977, but the window at the end of the corridor was so dirty that it might as well have been twilight. The door was plain, and only the simple sign that read *Indigo Wagstaff, CI* told me that I was in the right place. It was plastic, not brass, so Wagstaff was either stingy, poor, or thought that the sign was only temporary. None of these possibilities filled me with vast amounts of confidence. I knocked anyway.

After a minute or so, the door was opened by a man in his early thirties. He looked as I expected – brown hair hanging loose and unstyled, just slightly longer than shoulder length, a thick beard, longer and just as uncared for, flared jeans and an orange silk shirt, unbuttoned and hanging loose, exposing his chest – skinny, pale and hairy, with a pentangle pendant on a heavy silver chain poking out from the scraggy end of his beard. He wiped his lips with the back of his hand then pushed his hair back. His eyes were piercing blue, fiercely intelligent, his pupils slightly dilated. He glanced at me as if I was nothing, not even worth a moment of attention.

I was wearing my smartest frock, so this annoyed me.

"What do you want?" he asked.

I cleared my throat. "Mr. Wagstaff?" I asked, and he nodded. "I find myself at your doorstep in need of the services of an investigator."

"Cool. Well, you better come in then, grab a seat or whatever. And call me Indigo. All my friends call me Indigo."

His office was simple: a desk, two chairs, a side table, a filing cabinet. There was a door to a second room; a bedroom from the glimpse I caught as I sat down. I made myself as comfortable as I could in one of the worn leather chairs. He put Bowie's *Low* on the record player and turned the volume down so we could talk.

"So I have two questions," he said as he sat and started buttoning up his shirt. "And these are the easy ones. There will be difficult ones later, but it's not a test. Except when it is a test. Firstly, why exactly do you require an investigator?" He leaned forward, and his hair fell over his face, so he pushed it back again.

"And secondly?"

He tutted and waved a finger at me in remonstration. "Now, now, miss. First question first, second question after," he paused, with his finger in the air. "Maybe more questions after that. We'll see how it goes. That's generally how this sort of thing works, isn't it?"

"It's Victoria. She's my friend." I realised that wasn't quite right. "More than just a friend really, I guess. She…well, she's in trouble. I don't know where she is. That's not like her. I just know she's in trouble. But…"

"But it's not been long enough for the police to get involved, so you thought you'd come to someone who might do something? That's the usual story."

"Yes," I nodded. "And also, because…because it could be nothing yet. I don't know. Do you ever get feelings like that Mr. Wagstaff – Indigo? Premonitions?"

"Which brings us nicely to our second question, I suspect. Which is why, exactly, did you pick me?"

I gave this a little thought while he stared at me with that penetrating gaze. His lips were tight, his expression serious. My answer clearly mattered to him. I heard movement in the room next door but didn't look away from Indigo. I found myself wishing I had something to say, something that would satisfy him.

"I don't know," I admitted eventually. "I just sort of turned up here."

"So you just came to me because it felt right?"

"Yes," I admitted, with what I hoped was a faintly sheepish smile.

He broke into a delighted grin. "That's just perfect! Absolutely perfect!"

I raised an eyebrow, and he continued. "Because what I do, right, it's kind of mystical, if you get my drift. I investigate physically, for sure, but also astrally. I'm always working on many planes, all at once. And we're all connected, you know?"

I nodded. I hadn't had cause to use an investigator before, but I was aware of the methods involved. Ever since the summer of '67 there had been an explosion in the psychedelic sciences and while they weren't exactly mainstream yet, it was only a matter of time before they pervaded everyday life. My parents still thought it was all about drugs and sex and, to be fair, most of it was. But the practical uses were starting to emerge, mainly in medicine and entertainment, while there were rumours of the American army setting up a paranormal paramilitary.

"So what I suspect is that you came to me because I am uniquely positioned to help you," he continued.

The door to what was now confirmed as Indigo's bedroom opened, and the man I assumed was his lover came in with a mug of something steamy and vaguely pungent.

"I heard you talking, Indy," he said. "I thought you'd like some tea." He looked at me as he put the mug down. "I didn't make any for your guest. Should I?"

Indigo picked up the tea and swigged it down.

"I don't think so," he said. "We're just leaving."

"Oh."

The two kissed, and Indigo gave his lover a cheeky pat on the bottom as he went back – presumably to bed.

"I would have introduced you," he said to me quietly once the door was closed. "But I've never found out his name and it's reached the point where asking would be really, really awkward. This, by the way, is mushroom tea. You're welcome to join me in some after this is over, but for now I need you to be firmly grounded while I can be a bit more exploratory. Shall we go?"

And with that he bustled me out of the office. I still had many questions, but I doubted he would answer them. There was something about him that I found myself trusting innately. His breath smelled of thyme and mushroom and his hand felt right in mine. He was, however, very annoying.

Halfway down the stairs he stopped me.

"Where are we going?" he asked. "I knew there would be more questions. And that's quite a good one. It's not quite as good as asking how much you're going to pay me for my services, but you're very pretty and I can be very flexible, so I was planning on saving that one for later, once we have found your friend."

There was something about the way that he said *friend* that I found a little unsettling. I looked blankly at him for a moment before I realised that he had asked where we were going.

"Stockwell," I said.

He raised his head as if sniffing the air. "That's amazing." Without further explanation, he pulled me down the remaining stairs. Before I knew it, we were in Warren Street Tube station.

"The thing that I love about this station," he explained, unprompted, "is that it is just so London. Know what I mean?"

I didn't. He could tell that. He took a deep breath.

"OK. So they built the station about seventy years ago. They rebuilt it twenty-five years later, adapted it, put in escalators. But times changed and the station needed to change too, so they did a bit more refurbishment, not as severe, must've been about nine, ten years ago. And there was outrage about it too, massive complaints from the locals when they put in the barriers. Nowadays we just swan through them, don't we? We barely even notice them. But all that history, it's still written here, if you know where to look for it. Sometimes it's subtle, and sometimes it's a little more obvious."

We had reached the Northern Line platform by this stage, and we stopped next to a section of the wall where the words Euston Road were set in the tiling.

"They only called the station Euston Road for a year," he explained. "And they changed it. I've no idea why. But they left the signs of what it had been. And that's a metaphor."

"For London?"

"For everywhere in general, but for London in particular."

"I see."

"No, you don't."

He was absolutely right. So I tried to change the subject.

"Is that why we're on the Northern Line then? Are we here so that you could show me that sign and make your point?"

"No. Well, yes, partly, but not really. We're taking the Northern Line so I don't get confused, and because we get to go through Waterloo, which I always love because it's such a silly name. And there's some bad energy around Green Park that I'm trying to avoid. Karma is not good there and hasn't been for a couple of days so I'm trying to steer clear. But mainly, it's the confusion."

"Confusion?" The train arrived. Not as busy as I thought it might be at this time of the evening; I guessed the commuter rush hour must be pretty much over.

"Yes! You see, when we get to Stockwell, I'm going to try to find Victoria. If I take the Victoria line I might find the wrong Victoria by mistake. I could end up anywhere. I might even end up back here, which would be rather tiresome. Got to keep my Victorias separate. Do you get me?"

"No," I said, emphatically. "I really don't."

"Everything is interconnected." He left it there as if that explained everything. I tried to read the adverts above the windows as the train trundled under London, but it was jolting so much that I couldn't focus and the words jumbled together. Indigo was mercifully quiet for a couple of minutes, but started talking again as we pulled out of Embankment.

"You've got an A to Z, haven't you?"

"Everyone does."

"And that helps you get from place to place. It's like a network. It makes connections. It helps you understand. But on the back page there's another map, another network."

"That's just the Tube map."

"But think about it because it's really cool. You've got two maps, linking the same places, but they're entirely different. And they're at different levels, one below the other. And the Tube lines, they criss-cross and intertwine. There's so much going on above the ground and under the ground and yet you can get the whole of London into a book that's small enough to fit in to your pocket, and all of the underground onto a single sheet. It's amazing when you think about it. And that's just in the A to Z. London has so many maps, all superimposed on each other like they're drawn on tracing paper. Did you know there used to be almost two dozen rivers in London, and you could follow them just like you can walk along a street? They're all underground now, mostly in the sewers, but they're like the Euston Road sign. There are still signs there if you know where to find them. And then there are the secret maps, ley lines and dragon lines deep in the earth, and lines of astral force in the sky, and everywhere the lines meet is a person or a place or a time. And you know what? I can see them all. And they all have so many Victorias. I need to be sure I find the right one."

"OK," I said, after he paused for breath. "I get it. You didn't want to go on the Victoria Line because it interferes with the magic. I get that. That's fine. It's just it's usually quicker. So that's why I thought getting the Northern Line was odd."

"It's not magic," he replied huffily. "It's just science we don't fully understand yet."

He looked like I had hurt his feelings, so I put my arm around him and gave him what I hoped was a reassuring squeeze. "If it helps any, I do have a feeling you're going to find her."

"Don't worry about that," he smiled. "I'm definitely going to find her. The only question is whether I will find her in time."

The sun was setting when we left the station at Stockwell. By then, I had been informed that Stockwell was one of the first deep level underground stations and that this was, in some sense, significant. Indigo hadn't explained exactly why, and I didn't exactly care, so hadn't paid attention even if he had told me. I was sure that if it became important, he would take great delight in telling me again.

For all his bluster there was something about his self-confidence that I found reassuring. Even when he pulled out a pair of sunglasses with mismatched lenses and put them on despite the twilight not being bright enough to merit them, I felt that they gave him an air of gravitas, and that they served some purpose. They probably let him see things that weren't visible to the naked eye. That seemed plausible, or nonsense. Definitely one or the other.

Victoria's flat was just across the road, and her spare key was under the flowerpot, as usual.

His words were decidedly getting to me. I had been acutely aware that the escalator had taken us from one version of the city to another, and I had been feeling increasingly uneasy the closer we got to the flat. I let Indigo go inside and upstairs first. He had insisted, declaring, "I shall go first, just in case. You're already worried enough, and there could be anything in there. These eyes have seen many things that a young lady ought not to see," which I found to be a little patronising and decidedly chauvinistic. However, on balance, I was reassured.

He unlocked the door and went in, closing it behind him. I waited on the landing, looking at the door, listening. It seemed to take an age, but when he opened it again, I saw that he had taken his glasses off and he had a forced smile which I suspected was an effort to look reassuring. "She's not here."

I was relieved. I hadn't been sure what to expect, signs of struggle, a note, a body, even. But there was nothing. Victoria's flat was as tidy and ordered as ever.

"How well do you know this flat?" he asked me.

"Very well," I replied.

"Good."

At his suggestion, we checked the flat methodically. He observed and commented on everything, but mainly on trivial things that I wouldn't have thought of. The kettle was cold, there was only one mug in the sink, the milk was fresh. Her bed was made, the scent of joss sticks was apparently fresh enough for him to be sure that they had been lit within the last twelve hours. I looked at the bookcases and didn't see anything that looked unfamiliar or obviously missing except for Victoria's treasured book of Arthurian legends which wasn't in its usual place on the shelf between the *Bhagavad Gita* and *The Female Eunuch*. We found it a few minutes later under the spare toilet roll on the windowsill in the bathroom.

"She keeps a tidy flat," Indigo noted eventually. "Which gives us some comfort, but also a dearth of clues. I can tell that she's about the same age as you, has a similar hair colour, likes the occasional cigarette, and also a joint now and then. But she doesn't really approve of them and doesn't

94

like the fact that she does it. It makes her feel weak. She is sceptical about the new metasciences and is trying to find ways to make herself believe, because she really wants to. She feels increasingly outcast in the world. She is surrounded by the children of the revolution but feels that it has passed her by. She'd be more comfortable in tweed than a kaftan, but she sees the new world with jealousy. I'd guess she would have been about fourteen during the first summer of love, and hates that she was young enough to want to join in, but not old enough to do so. She reminds me of you. Have you known her long?"

"As long as I can remember."

"I thought you'd say something like that. Was I close?"

"Yes."

"That's a relief. I was making most of it up. Do you know where she keeps the other books?"

That surprised me. He was right, Victoria had other books, and I knew where she kept them. "How do you…" I began.

"One of them will be *The Joy of Sex*," he explained. "Everybody has a copy, but a nice young lady like Victoria, or yourself, wouldn't have it out on show just in case she had company. She wouldn't want any man she brought home to think that she was some sort of tramp, but she would want to know what to do. So it's probably quite well read. And probably near her bed."

"There's a squeaky floorboard in the bedroom that comes loose, just by the wardrobe. It's under there."

There were two books in the hidden cavity. As predicted, a well-thumbed copy of *The Joy of Sex*, and a very tatty copy of Augustine's *Transubstantiation Through Love*. There was also a business card for Indigo Wagstaff CI, Intuitive Detective, which I must have seen before but somehow forgotten about.

"Have you read this?" he asked, waving Augustine's book at me.

"A couple of times," I admitted.

"It's a work of genius," he continued. "Deeply flawed, but he really gets it. Mainly he's trying to get his leg over with as many women, or men, as he can, but he stumbles on a few things in there that I've seen. I mean, when he talks about opening the third eye to reveal the true self and the inner beauty he's talking about sex, because there's no such thing as a third eye. But when he talks about building bridges between the levels of the universe, he's pretty spot on. And when he talks about a worm eating itself, you can read that as embracing the cyclical nature of reality, but I'm pretty sure he's talking about sex again. That's the problem with the metasciences. It's very easy to get them confused with wish fulfilment."

"Have you finished?" I asked. He looked a little sheepish.

"Yes. But this is good. It's important to her. She keeps it safe, and she keeps it secret. It will do nicely. Are you ready?"

"Ready?"

"We're going on another trip."

"Where to?"

"I don't know," he explained, with a glint in his eye. "Isn't that exciting?"

He looked crazy. And I was excited.

Indigo drew a chalk pentangle on the kitchen floor and placed one of Victoria's possessions at each vertex, the ash from her incense, hair tugged from her hairbrush, her favourite mug, some of her underwear rescued from the laundry basket, and the copy of *Transubstantiation of Love*, open at the page where it fell naturally. He boiled the kettle and started to make some tea from honey and some chopped mushrooms that he took from a bag on the inside pocket of his overcoat. He rang a small bell while the mushrooms infused.

"It doesn't do anything," he explained. "I just like the noise."

After a few minutes, he strained the tea into a second mug. We sat next to each other, cross-legged on the floor. I asked if I should sit in the lotus position.

"You can if you want. It doesn't make any difference.

Close your eyes."

I did so and heard Indigo swigging down the tea, then felt his hand in mine. I was surprised by the warmth of it, and by the softness of his palm. And then, while I knew we were still sitting on the kitchen floor, we were also stepping forward into the pentangle.

"How…?"

"I'm extending my aura," he said, as if that explained anything. "We're walking onto the astral plane together. Keep hold of my hand, I don't want to lose you. If you feel me fading away, call out my name."

It occurred to me at that moment that I barely knew this man, and that he didn't even know my name. And that we were now at the point where asking me would be really, really awkward. We stepped through the pentangle into Trafalgar Square.

It wasn't quite Trafalgar Square – rainbow tinges to everything. The tourists were pigeons, and the pigeons were tourists. Horatio Nelson sat atop his column, brushing dried guano from his shoulders as it rose and fell – sometimes high above us and at others low enough to reach out and touch him.

Victoria, in her summer hat, kicking through the fountains, posing for a photograph for a tourist-pigeon. I remember that day. We had finished work early, sneaked out and gone to the pub. We'd met the photographer who said he would make us the face of 1977, and he'd taken pictures of us in his studio and we'd smoked something. And he'd suggested we go out. At this moment, as we were dancing in the square, we had felt like we were the embodiment of London.

This wasn't my memory, I realised. It was Victoria's. For her, this was the world in that moment, her alone, in the fountain, in the sky with Nelson, in London. Nobody else mattered. The photographer was just another pigeon, as I assumed I was too. He didn't matter, in the same way that we wouldn't matter to him beyond one o'clock the next morning when he would roll off Victoria and tell her that he needed to go home before his wife's shift ended.

"It's not even really her memory," explained Nelson, hopping off his column and taking my other hand. "It's the truth of it, though. It's the important version. Look at the lions."

I looked at the lions. They appeared to be like cartoons. The nearest one winked at me and grinned.

"Why are we here?" asked Indigo.

"It's the beginning, Indigo," Nelson explained. "Not hugely important, mind you. But it's the first time they meet."

And then there was someone else there – someone I had forgotten about. A handsome man in green cords and a green shirt, short curly chestnut hair and a tight beard reached out to grasp Victoria's hand as she stumbled. For an instant, I was looking at him through Victoria's eyes, feeling trust and safety. And then he was gone.

"Is that who she's with?" I asked. And then I realised I didn't need to. "That *is* who she's with."

"Who is he?" asked Indigo.

"Come with me," replied Nelson.

He led us through an invisible angle and onto a new plane.

We turned into not quite Leicester Square, surrounded by walls of posters competing to advertise *Jabberwocky* and *The Lord of the Rings*. Victoria and the man in green were on a bench in the gardens, holding hands and watching the trees grow.

"What is a Jabberwocky?" he asked.

"Something from a kid's book," explained Victoria.

I remembered that day too. The man from Trafalgar Square was still wearing green. His beard was a little longer, starting to tangle. Victoria was wearing slacks and a candy-striped blouse, unbuttoned to a daring level.

"And a Lord of the Rings?"

"The same."

"Is everything about children's stories now?"

Victoria shrugged. "I think people find a truth in them

98

that's appealing. It's an escape from the everyday."

"That's strange. We should grow out of childish things. But I can see why you would want to escape this…place."

"Oh," said Victoria, folding her arms defensively in the same way that I did. "I don't want to escape London. It's the most exciting place in the world."

He chuckled. "It always has been," he said. He had a translucency to him, I noticed, almost a transparency. I knew his face well, but I didn't know where from. Victoria gave him a peck on the cheek, squeezed his hand, and he seemed slightly more real, slightly more present.

"Who is he?" I asked, as much to myself as anyone else. I was barely aware of Indigo and Nelson's hands in mine. I squeezed them both, hoping it would make me feel less transparent.

"Who are you?" Victoria asked him.

"You wouldn't believe me if I told you," he said.

"I might."

"Come with me."

Nelson tugged us sideways.

A church. We were standing in the nave, and the Green Man was showing Victoria a carving – a face carved into the leaf decorations at the top of a column. It had branches for hair, leaves for a beard and eyes that were familiar.

"Is that you?" Victoria asked.

"It's a memory of me," he replied. "I was here before there were people in London. I was a god, then, perhaps, or the beginnings of the idea of a god. I was like a tree. I spread out across the countryside. I gave sustenance and support and fruit and shelter, and I was loved. It was a good time. The people respected the land and the land respected the people and I was part of that."

Victoria gave him a peck on the cheek.

"So you believe me?" he asked.

"I don't know," she replied. "But it's like a lot of the things you read now, about how we need to get back to nature, respect the planet. Flower power, you know?" She had a rainbow aura, sparkling.

"He's talking gibberish," I said to Nelson. He looked at me and raised an eyebrow.

"There are many truths," said Indigo. "This is his, or at least a version of it. And look, she believes him."

I'd believed him too, at the time. But I was annoyed that I didn't feature anywhere in Victoria's memory.

Indigo nodded to Nelson, who snapped his fingers. The floor opened up beneath the three of us and we fell upwards, folding in on ourselves.

In a dingy bedsit, two men are seated on an unmade bed. The older one has his arm around the younger.

"This isn't Victoria's memory," I said.

"This is wrong," added Indigo.

"This is a shortcut," explained Nelson. "I think."

As we watched, the older man put a square of paper on his tongue and leaned in, his hand on the younger man's thigh.

"Is that you?" I asked Indigo. The tear in his eye told me it was.

As the two men kissed, and the older man slipped his hand towards Indigo's crotch, there was a sense of separation, and I saw the two men stepping out of their bodies, their presence moving on one plane while also staying in place. I saw the levels, the layers of existence. And then the colour began to drain out of this version of the world. There were no rainbows, just shades of purple. Even the older man had gone now, and young Indigo, fading, reached out for himself. And we stepped through him.

"That wasn't fair, Nelson," he said, once we had our breath back.

"I know." Nelson grinned. "But it was the fastest memory to get us here."

Indigo glared at Nelson, who muttered something about non-linear mapping on the astral plane.

Here was a bench on Clapham Common. It was misty, the air was moist, and the trees stretched over us like the vaults of a church. I knew why we were there. It was the night when Victoria and the Green Man split up.

And there they were, just where I knew they would be. She came marching down the path, her coat pulled around her. He was behind her, shouting, chasing after her. He reached out and his arm seemed unnaturally long as he clasped his hand to her shoulder. She stopped, turned to face him. As I knew she would, she reached out to slap him, and he grabbed her wrist before she could hit him.

"Why won't you believe me?" he asked.

"Oh, I believe you," she said. "I really do. I believe that you think you're an ancient god, woken from a 'deep slumber' by a new bunch of hippies trying to get back to nature. I believe that you look at the world and see the damage we've done, and it grieves you, and you want to help us sweep it all away. But mainly, I believe that you're a manipulative piece of shit. Go back to whichever nuthouse you crawled out of and tell them to increase your dosage because you're seriously fucked up. Now leave me alone. Just go. Go!"

I turned to Indigo, puzzled. "I remember that. But I wasn't there, was I? I can't have been."

Victoria was alone now. Her God had forsaken her. He had faded away, even as I felt Nelson's fingers slipping through mine.

"We need to go back now, Victoria," said Indigo.

He hadn't asked my name because he had always known it, I realised. I wasn't really there, not on the same plane, not in the same version of reality. I looked at myself on the path, remembered what had happened next, and let Indigo Wagstaff pull me back to the real world with him.

I wasn't far away. I finally remembered setting up the wooden cross in the empty flat downstairs. It was part of a ritual that I had read in Augustine's book, a book that the Green Man had given me. The ritual was to summon and bind a god, it had said. But it seemed that wasn't exactly true.

I told Indigo the location and where the spare key was and

he hurled himself out of my flat and down the stairs. He didn't stop to look for the key, but gave the door a sharp kick next to the lock and it sprang open, the wood splintering slightly. I followed him, aware of how insubstantial I felt. I remembered coming in to the flat earlier that day, lighting the incense, preparing myself to summon him. It would be just for one final confrontation, I thought, to clear the air, to let him know who was in control.

I had been wrong. So wrong.

We looked at my body, tied down by thick vines that seemed to be growing out of the floor, at the tendrils that were plunging into me, through my thighs and my chest, where my flesh was taking on a lurid green hue. The rose grew where my mouth should be. The tendrils merged with my arms.

"What do you want?" asked Indigo.

My body twitched and wriggled, the tendrils writhed, the rose in my mouth retreated.

"To return," I said. These were not my words. His voice was speaking through me. He sounded petulant.

"And you're stealing this girl's body to do it? That seems a little bit insensitive. Not cool, man. Not cool."

The Green Man smirked. "She believes in me. It's all I need."

Indigo laughed at the Green Man. "So let me get this right. You're an ancient god, native to these parts, and you're like a tree, or a giant weed or something, and you've got roots spread out, all over London?"

"That's a simplification, but it's close enough."

"Please don't interrupt me while I'm summarising. It really interrupts my flow and it's kind of rude. I'm trying to keep this mellow here."

"You asked a question. I simply answered it." He was making me look smug. I didn't look good smug.

"The question was rhetorical. Anyway, the people worship you and then they start to build sewers, and roads, and railway lines on top of you. And all of these maps sit on you too, force you down, and you are forgotten." He paused. "It must have been awful for you."

"I lived, slept, deep in the earth, in dreams, in memories. Occasionally they thought of me, and then forgot me. But they didn't believe in me."

"I cannot imagine how that must have felt. But then we come along, the beautiful people, the children of the revolution. We look at the world we have made, we reject it, and we want to get back to nature. And suddenly you've got a way back, a way up to the surface again. And you find Victoria, who believes. But she is a bit rubbish, really. No offence—"

"None taken," I replied.

"And you think that she will be the first of your new followers, will bring you back. But the thing is that you need a body. And you can't take her body, can you? You can't kill your first new believer – your only new believer. After all, what is a god without a church? So you talk her into this ritual – no, you goad her into it. You make her think she will be punishing you, but actually she will be setting you free. That's it, isn't it?"

The Green Man wrinkled my face into an unflattering sneer.

"It was easy enough. She was weak, thought she was nothing. I gave her someone to believe in. And then I gave her the illusion of control, of power. And it's not like I'm asking for much from her. Just her body. I'm doing her a favour, really. She exists solely on the astral plane now. She's immortal, the first of my new followers."

And I remembered the feeling of him forcing himself into my body, forcing me out, sending me out into the world, amnesiac, my thoughts racing up the Victoria Line to Warren Street, out into the world of sorts, lost and alone.

"The thing is," continued Indigo, "I said that Victoria's a bit rubbish. And you said she was weak. But she's not really. She's smart, and brave, and actually pretty clever. She came to me because she was lost, and all I did was help her find her way here. At the end of the day, it's still her body, not yours. She can take it back any time she wants."

I stepped forward then, through Indigo, and reached out towards my hand. Contact tingled, and I felt so much pain – the agony of every cell in my body being torn apart and replaced. I screamed, and felt myself trying to leave my body again, but forced myself to stay, to reunite. He couldn't take my body by force without killing me. And without me he couldn't survive in my body. I felt him struggle and relent.

I don't know exactly what happened next. Back in my own body I felt amazing, strong and powerful, intensely aware of my breathing and my heart beating, and then realised I had lost a lot of blood and was in incredible pain. I blacked out, and when I came round, I was lying on the floor and felt like I had been in a fight. I had a hell of a headache. There were scars on my wrists and neck and ankles and thighs. But I was alive. I was myself again and I was alone.

I pulled the door to the downstairs flat closed and hoped that nobody would notice.

We meet for a coffee a few weeks later near Vauxhall, at the point where the river Effra flows into the Thames. I am wearing my Tweed jacket, Indigo in denim. His boyfriend is sitting in the corner, looking rough. It's Sunday morning, and I suspect they've been out all night. I still don't know Indigo's boyfriend's name and decide it would be really awkward to ask.

We indulge in small talk for a few minutes. I tell him I am feeling great, even though I am not entirely sure that is true. He tells me he is working on a new case involving the wife and son of a minor peer but that it is all very hush-hush. Eventually we talk about what happened to me.

"There are a few things I don't understand," I say. "I know he needed my spirit to be alive so he could take my body, but surely he just needed a believer. It could be any believer. And you believe in him."

Indigo smiles.

"I believe in a whole lot of crap, Victoria. Most of it contradicts itself. I generally just make stuff up as I go along. I certainly don't worship anyone except myself, I guess."

"That's not a bad way to be," I say.

He takes the Victoria Line. I take the bridge across the river. We are both heading north. Our paths cross again and again, above and below; tapestry threads woven through each other's lives.

Alan Taylor works with numbers during the day and words in his spare time. Born in Edinburgh, he has lived and worked in Hong Kong, Dublin and London, and is currently quite happily back in Edinburgh, where he lives with his husband. He dabbles in  photography, cooking and planning global domination (badly).

His writing is mainly short stories – he likes to write SFF, sometimes in other people's universes, but increasingly he likes to explore the alternative paths that history never took.

He can be found on twitter as @**alan_is_writing**, even when he isn't writing.

Follow Alan's Blog: **www.alaniswriting.wordpress.com**

Moon Dagger

Marie Gault

Sam Coates checks his watch, looks to the sky, then to the river, and nods. He is satisfied. Another thirty minutes and they can pack up.

He casts his eyes around his charges. A good morning's mudlarking. He smiles. Trowels busy but still secured to their waist cords. Everyone occupied. That's how he likes it. Wandering among the digging figures, he checks each bucket with an encouraging word. All good. Each bucket filling up nicely with old broken clay pipes and the occasional animal bell or pieces of broken glass.

He wanders over to Philip and peers into the boy's bucket. Something catches his eye. "Wait a minute! Is that a George V penny?" He motions to the boy to give him the coin and turns it over and over. Difficult to tell since it has obviously been buffeted and tumbled with the ebb and flow of the tide. But the head of the king is just about visible. Can it be? Perhaps. One for later, he decides.

He nods to the boy. "Good man. Well done. Yes, I think you have something very interesting there Philip. Keep it safe." With an encouraging smile, he pats the boy on the shoulder.

Sam moves on, then stops as he realises that one girl has edged further towards the river. "Too close, Caitlyn," he calls out. "You're too close to the river. Move over here." His hand waves to the small pile of rocks that someone had built into a tower, one stone balancing precariously on top of the other. But the girl seems not to hear him as she digs slowly and carefully, loosening the grit and sand from an object buried deep in the lumps of dried mud and cluster of pebbles.

He treads carefully. The head teacher has not told him the full story of this girl's life. School policy. Don't encourage gossip. But how to help if you don't know the problem? And then, what if there isn't a problem? He sighs. *Must do better,* he vows silently. *Must observe more closely and listen with the eyes, not just the ears.*

As he shakes himself into sharp awareness, he realises she hasn't heard his caution. The gulls swoop around her but she doesn't move away.

"Caitlyn." His voice knifes through the air for a moment as he moves closer. "Caitlyn…" And then he stops. "What is it, Caity? What have you found?"

Still the girl does not answer but continues to ease her trowel around the shape. Sam slides to his knees and watches with increasing excitement as his eyes follow the movement of her trowel.

He moves closer. "Ttttt," he mutters, and his fingers flicker furiously as he indicates this and that to the girl. She follows his line of thought and moves the trowel precisely as he would himself. But his impatience is festering. He wants to see what she seems to have seen. His hand trembles but hers is perfectly focused. *It's as if she knows*, he thinks as he moves his stare from the trowel to her face. She knows what is buried under the ground, he realises with a start.

"Sir, you told us to be gentle when we're excavating, so…" her voice drifts off to a whisper, "so I'm being gentle," she finishes. "There." She smiles up at him. "I think that's it uncovered." Once more, she bends her head to the ground. "Hmmm. It looks like a knife, sir." She continues to stare at the object. "I'm not quite sure but…" she pauses. "Actually, maybe it's a dagger. Could it be? Do you think?" She looks directly at him, her voice full of excitement. "It is a dagger, isn't it?" Her body gives an involuntary shiver. "A dagger from the past!"

A dagger? For Sam, the word throws out images redolent of warfare yet evocative of beauty. His hand moves slowly to his face. He trembles. Sharply, he jerks himself back to reality. "Here, let's have a look. Let me…" He stretches out his hand but too late. Little by little and with surprising delicacy, the girl is gently easing the object from the grasp of the foreshore. Then, cradling the trowel in her hand, she holds the find out for inspection.

Sam pulls out his empty snack-box from his rucksack, quickly lines it with a wad of tissues and, nodding to the girl, says, "Can you keep it on your trowel and slide it into the box? Gently, gently," he breathes as it slowly slips from the trowel. Relief escapes his lips and forms into a smile.

He gazes and gazes down at her find. *Control, Sam, control*, he urges his shaking body as he firstly uses his thumb-nail to chip away the detritus of millennia from the long, thin object. Now he wets his finger and smears it over the remains of the river mud. Finally, he takes a tissue from his pocket and smooths it over the blade. As he does so, a burnished glow arises, dull at first, but then glorious. A long, low thread of air whistles from his lips.

He lifts his head and smiles at the girl, and with a nod, he wets his finger again and strokes it lightly over the handle. Intricate animal patterns begin to reveal themselves. His whole body trembles. He grips the box tightly, controls his shaking and bites his lower lip thoughtfully. Then he looks into the girl's eager eyes.

"Caitlyn," he begins slowly, "Caitlyn, I think you've found something very important."

Her face radiates success. And there is an indefinable quality about that look. It has depth. It comes from somewhere deep inside her being.

Sam smiles and he too shares that success. This girl has an instinct for excavation; an appreciation for and an understanding of the past. "Well done, Caitlyn," he says, his praise honest and sincere.

She bubbles with excitement and reaches out her hand to grasp the dagger.

"No, no," he warns. "It's dangerous."

She shrinks back, gasps and shivers.

Damn, his brain registers. *I've ruined her excitement.*

"No, no. It's OK. Look," and he touches the jagged tip of the weapon. "Sharp! I'm just protecting you."

She nods and takes a step backwards, stretches out her neck and circles her head just long enough to catch a glint of the burnished surface of the blade. She moves forward again. Closer. Even closer. Her gasp is full of awe. The others hear and clatter their buckets down onto the pebbles of the foreshore as they push each other forward to see the find.

"Stand well back and I'll let you look when I've cleaned off more of the dirt," Sam instructs. "No, don't crowd me in." His voice rings sharper now. "Just be patient." His hand waves them away as he laughs. Ten-year-olds are not the most patient of creatures.

Still holding the dagger-box, he looks at each child in turn. "We've got about ten minutes left before your parents arrive. Yes? So I suggest we sit over there, nearer to the road," he waves his arm towards the embankment, "and then I'll clean the dagger some more. Hopefully, I'll be able to tell you more about it then. After that, we should take it to the Museum of London and report its location." Seven solemn heads nod at this instruction.

"Sir, is it very valuable?" Charlie asks.

"Could be priceless, Charlie. We'll let the experts decide."

There is a collective whistle of appreciation and shouts of "What about a reward?" … "Will we be on TV?" … "I'm going to be an archaeologist." … "Me too, me too." …

There is a chorus of agreement. The excitement is palpable.

Sam laughs and turns to Philip. "Right, Philip. Lead the way, please."

"Sir, what's that noise?" Caitlyn halts suddenly.

"What noise?" He stops for a second and looks around. "Oh, it's just the traffic. We're right beside the main road, remember. Come on, let's go. Keep moving. Keep moving." He urges the snaking line forward.

"No, sir," the girl stops again, narrows her eyes and holds her head as if smelling for the sound. "It sounds like someone crying. Let's look," she urges Sam. "Maybe they need help."

"Caitlyn, it's the breeze. Just the breeze. Now come on." He waves his arm impatiently. "Over there, in the shelter under the wooden props, please. Keep moving." He pauses for a split second, counts the heads and, satisfied he still has seven youngsters, ushers them towards the overhang.

***

But Caitlyn is persistent. "There it's again." She tugs the arm of the girl in front. "Can you not hear it, Rosie?" she whispers.

"Sir said it's just the breeze," Rosie whispers back. "Come on. I want to see your dagger." Rosie tries to grasp her hand, but Caitlyn feels an energy, a frightening force pushing her back.

She doesn't seem to hear Rosie's words. Instead, she looks back towards the river and, beyond its long stretch, sees a movement of the thin reeds...

***

The reeds parted and a girl called Eved looked round. She thought she'd heard voices, but no one was there. She looked skyward but only two seabirds swooped across the spreading river. They squawked and screamed as they dived to the ground, and she shuddered and turned back to hide in the reeds, but her dress was weighed down by the mud and it dragged heavily around her ankles. Her once-beautiful cloak had slipped but she tugged it back into position over her thin shoulders. Then she fingered the skin pouch. If that was safe, all was well.

Crouching low, she looked at her bleeding legs but felt no pain, just deadness. The thin hide that covered her feet was worn and torn and gave no resistance to the sludge. Its squelch tried to suck her down. She would have to find another pathway to survival. A soft cry escaped her lips...

***

Caitlyn hears a cry coming from the reeds. She stops and looks to the sky. The seagulls are wheeling round and round, but their cry is a different cry. She takes slow, reluctant steps towards the others as they make their way to the overhang, but with every other step she stops and glances over her shoulder. She is aware of Mr. Coates waving to her, and she hears him call her name. She opens her mouth to reply, but a breeze whips up from nowhere and freezes her lips.

Even so, her head can turn. And slowly it does. She sees again the golden light of the dagger as it lay in the ground. She sees that same light as an almost dissolving pillar of smudged brightness. It tries to enclose her whole being until she too becomes the golden light. And it hurts. Like a rope twisting round her fingers. Like a knife carving into her hand, she finds the pain unbearable.

"Push the light away. Push the light away." Each syllable is enunciated more forcibly than the previous one. She thrusts her hands stiffly before her for protection and forces her head back to look at the other children.

Rosie is trying to run towards her, but her legs just move slowly and stiffly. The other children are waving her back to them, but little by little, their faces begin to merge into the shadow of the noonday sun. A ghosting image. Grainy. Outlines fading. She is losing them. She tries to take a step forward…

***

Eved's foot struck something hard and she was glad of the hurt. It nudged her into resistance. They would not catch her. She forced her legs forward, pushing them away from the mud, thrusting her arms through the reeds, straining her eyes through the sharp slant of the sun.

Then she stopped and listened. There was a bark. A snarl. A threatening snarl. And then a deep throated growl. It was the wolf. They had brought the animal, the wolf. It would track her, smell her redness, smell her *boladh*. She fingered her pouch again. Yes, the dagger was still there. She would use it if she had to.

Pushing forward, she found the reeds had thickened. Noiselessly, she slid to the ground. Harder here, the ground was pitted with stones and gravel, and it cut into her skin, but no redness ran out. She was safe. For the present at least. She rubbed her arm, the arm with the marks from the metal; the marks of swirls and interlocking leaves which reminded her of the great trees. The great trees of the forests of her childhood. She remembered when the burning rod had cooled, and the pain had gone from her arm. She remembered she had tried to rub off the marks, but they were engraved into her flesh. Burned with the thin tracery of the new metal. Like a birth mark…

Her grandmother was speaking to her…

"Eved, they can burn your arm, but they cannot steal your anam. *Resist! You are special." And she touched Eved's forehead with the purple-headed flower that promised healing and protection. Then she showered some of its burned, dried leaves over her head.*

Eved listened and began to understand. She looked into her grandmother's face and saw the wisdom, but she also saw the fear.

Slowly and consciously, she stared into her grandmother's eyes and continued the search for the answer, the answer to her grandmother's fear, the answer to her own fear.

As the old lady's faded blue eyes grew larger and larger, swimming with tears, Eved held contact so that she might discover the truth. Her grandmother rubbed the purple-headed flower between her fingers and released its pungent scent. The odour filled Eved's senses and gradually, she witnessed the old woman pulsate into an image of youthful beauty. That which had been old, had grown young. This young woman smiled and let her fingers ripple through her long dark hair. She tossed that hair and laughed. Oh how she laughed! Eved heard that laughter. Laughter like a gurgle of water bubbling over the stones in the river's shallows. Eved held her gaze until this woman, this young woman, dissolved into her own being, until they were as one.

But slowly, and very slowly, the young woman with the long dark hair began to crumble into sadness. No smiles, no more laughter. Instead there was a man, and now the man was laughing. He was pulling at the young woman's hair and twisting her face to his. His eyes grew black, and she began to cry.

Eved felt that pain within her own being. There was agony and distress as the man snarled into the woman's body. Eved stretched out her arm to help. She opened her mouth to call, but no words left her lips...

And what were words anyway? Nothing. The image slipped and slipped until Eved saw no more. She slumped to the floor of straw. Exhausted, the pictures ebbed away, but she refused to let them disappear completely.

Slowly and very slowly, Eved felt her grandmother's essence return. Piece by piece, the images began to re-frame and as they did, so too did she begin to understand what she had seen. She gathered her thoughts and called for strength. Her mind slipped into long-remembered words. She clung to their power...

Eved could hear her grandmother's voice giving her reassurance. "Your anam *is your spirit, Eved. Your spirit can never be destroyed. Even after you have passed, your spirit... this essence that is you...this will live forever. It has made you special."*

But Eved was losing her belief and so the power of the long-remembered words was slipping away from her. She could only see the growing savagery of the man and the desolation of the young woman, her young grandmother. Her hand reached out once more to help her grandmother but the space between them was too wide. Her grandmother was fading. Once more she stretched out, but the image had gone.

She clasped her head in her hands and cried out in anguish: "No, no, I want to live forever with you, matta... Forever, please. I do not want this man. Take him from me."

She could taste her own fear. She could touch that fear.

Previously, it had only been like the fluttering chill of the spring breeze; now it echoed the screech of the dark shadows that roamed the night-time land. And again, she pleaded, "Please, matta."

But the young grandmother had slipped away. Only her scent lingered, and this fragrance was absorbed by a blue, misty greyness that whirled around Eved. It billowed and billowed, swirled and spiralled until it formed the image of the old lady. In a moment, that old lady, her grandmother, turned her deeply troubled eyes from her.

***

The old lady knew she must protect her granddaughter from the sadness that still haunted her memory. She tried to open a space in her mind to allow her memory to find hope. She pleaded with silent words as she turned slowly to face the girl.

The girl stared unseeing, entranced, motionless.

Girl and grandmother in static harmony.

And then in her memory cell she saw it. The dagger. The treasured dagger. Her only possession. It had served her well.

Even so, as her memory found the dagger, a voice in the wind whirled through the air around her. "Do not give her the dagger," it whispered, and then blew sadly and heaved a sigh through the round house. Through the thatch it whistled sharply and then out through the crevice of reeds it whirled towards the clearing.

"With the dagger she might not survive," was the echo which trailed in its wake.

"But without the dagger she will be vulnerable. She must live."

Eved moved towards her. She outstretched her arms, hands waiting to clasp hers.

"She must live; she is my special one." Those words were spoken as if from a great distance, far removed from the girl.

"Listen to me," the voice in the wind returned, softly

scattering angelica in its wake. "She will be vulnerable with the dagger," it moaned. "You cannot give this great burden to one so young," it breathed.

"She will be vulnerable without the dagger." Her lips moved softly but with purpose. With those words, she moved towards Eved and surged strength back within her.

And so it was, with one last heave, the wind calmed in a great gasp: "Carnach," and then its strength was gone.

The old lady opened her tired eyes and looked at her granddaughter with an inconsolable flicker of pain. "I have reached the end of my first existence," her sad voice murmured to the girl. "My next time awaits. You must travel this journey on your own but my spirit is with your spirit, Eved."

Globules of silent tears ran from Eved's eyes, but the girl never wavered in her gaze towards her.

"I know now that our only hope is Carnach of the great water," the old lady continued. "If you can reach the water and make the offering, Carnach will help. Carnach always helps the special ones. We must prepare."

And so they had made preparation. She presented the little dagger to her granddaughter, and the girl wrapped it in leaves and placed it in her pouch...

***

Now as Eved stood at the meeting of the great waters, she fingered the pouch and heard her grandmother's voice drifting in and out on the breeze.

"Remember I am with you, Eved," it murmured.

Softly and gently, the words and their sound sank into her consciousness and she could almost taste its melodious lilt. Her grandmother's voice resonated in her head. "My special one. My special one," it seemed to whisper. "Cast the dagger into the swelling waters on the rise of the moon." And so the whisper drifted far and far, through the reeds, across the water, and beyond.

Eved's tears dried. She knew what she had to do. When

the time arrived she would let the dagger fly to Carnach. She breathed deeply and calmly, folded her arms over her head and curling down into a low crouch, she placed her hand firmly on the dagger. Soon the moon would rise for her.

She did not hear the men with the dog. She did not hear the dog. All was quiet. Yes, she could resist...

***

Caitlyn feels her resistance and she struggles to hold on to reality. She can feel a force dragging her towards the river. She knows the tide is turning. It swishes and gurgles as it churns down the channel.

"Caitlyn," Rosie's voice rings out. "Cait-lyn! Sir's going to tell us about the dagger." She rushes to Caitlyn and reaches out to grab her hand. But the hands cannot meet. There is a force pulling them apart.

Caitlyn shrinks back and, with a sudden thrust, pushes both arms tightly to her body. "Don't touch me. Don't touch me," she hisses. "Get away," her voice seems to snarl.

"Caitlyn," Rosie screams. And then her voice drops to a gasp. "Caitlyn, your arm. Look," and her hands fly to her face as she gazes with horror at Caitlyn's arm. "What... what...happened to it?" Rosie's voice quivers. "Those red circles!"

Caitlyn holds Rosie's gaze. Eternity passes. Then a spreading smile. A deep breath. And laughter.

"The red circles?"

The other nods and waits.

"That's my birthmark," Caitlyn says, taking the other girl's hand. "It comes up really red when I'm scared. My grandma says the mark makes me her special one."

They laugh and run off to join the others. Behind them, the Thames flows darkly, unmindful of shadows yet to come.

———————

Marie Gault graduated from Glasgow University with a degree in Scottish History, Sociology and English. She taught English Language and Literature in Scotland, London, and Prague, and was an examiner in English Lit for the International Baccalaureate exam.

Her first venture into creative writing was in the 90s when she co-wrote a play about the early Labour Party leader, Keir Hardie, which toured West of Scotland during the Glasgow City of Culture.

She has also contributed literary criticism to Voxlit under a pseudonym and is currently working on two novels.

The Eye

Tom Halford

Martin was exhausted.

He was beat.

He was so tired that he could barely see.

The flight from Halifax had been fine enough. He couldn't get comfortable, though. His back was tight. The guy next to him smelled like frayed wires and boiled eggs. He was too sleepy to focus on his book, *We Are the Weather,* and when he tried to watch a movie on the tiny screen, the crew kept interrupting with their announcements about seat belts and turbulence and other things.

The truth was that the flight was not fine at all. It was travel made into torture. He was too exhausted and drunk to be awake, but he was too uncomfortable to find any rest.

The morning after the flight, he had woken up in his hotel room and walked over to the minibar. The tiny bottles of whiskey, rum, and vodka were tempting, but he was sick of booze. He'd had enough on the flight over.

Instead, he opted for the complimentary box of cereal. He tore it open, poured it into a bowl, and held his cereal under the sink, dampening it with tap water, which was gross, yes, but Martin didn't care.

His granddaughter, Sheree, always put water on her cereal.

He could tell her that he had done the same when he got back to Canada.

Besides, he didn't know where he was going to get milk in London. He didn't know how much a carton of milk cost in London. He thought about it. He didn't even know if the English used the word *carton*. Did they have a different word? A trolley? A trolley of milk? That didn't sound right to him.

In any case, he couldn't deal with these variables, so he splashed tap water onto his bowl of cereal and began to crunch through the disgusting mush of sugar and carbohydrates.

He rubbed his eyes and tried to wake himself up.

Something in the bowl of cereal slowly came into vision. At first, it looked like an oversized marshmallow, a kind of white bulb in the grey brown mess. Then, as Martin rubbed his eyes harder, he saw that it looked more like a big, fat marble.

Martin blinked and pushed his face close to the bowl, squinting. He gasped and dropped the bowl onto the carpet. The spoon clanked against it as he realized what he had almost eaten.

Somehow, inexplicably, there was a human eye in his cereal. Had it come from the tap? Was it his own?

Instinctively, Martin reached for his face. He ran his fingers over both his eyes and looked in the mirror.

One of his own eyes had not fallen out of his head.

Whose eye was it?

Martin crouched on the floor and stared at the eyeball in the mush of cereal. He thought for a moment. Then he got a glass from the bathroom, filled it with cold water, walked back to the eye, and plunked the eye into the glass. There was something about water and moisture. He was sure that like a fish the eyeball needed to stay wet.

Otherwise, he was certain that the thing would die.

It felt strange.

He was holding a glass of water when he stepped out of

the elevator.

It felt particularly strange since the glass had an eyeball floating in it.

Originally, he had planned to phone the police and tell them about the eye, but something strange had happened while he was still in his room. From his window, the full scope of the city was in the distance; endless brick, concrete, glass, endless wealth and history.

This was the London that he'd read about since he was a small boy. This was where important things happened, where important people lived, where it seemed like the future was decided.

He'd held the glass up so he could get a better look at the eyeball, and that was the moment it happened. When he looked at the eyeball, it was as though he was also able to look through its pupil.

He saw the city as he did before, but now two numbers were superimposed over the top: 137 and 2018.

Somehow he also knew what the numbers meant.

There were 137 homicides in 2018.

He didn't know why he immediately knew how to interpret them, but it was clearly some capability of the eye.

It didn't just allow him to look. It guided him to a specific way of looking.

When Martin stepped out of the elevator, he had both hands on the glass, hiding the eyeball. He took a seat in the corner of the lobby and waited for someone interesting to observe.

A man walked in and surveyed the room. He was wearing a suit and was carrying a briefcase. He held up the glass with both hands and spread his fingers apart and looked at the man through the eye.

The first thing he noticed was that the man's face rounded off.

He had no nose.

Two words popped up when he looked at the man: white male.

Martin brought the eyeball down from his face and looked

at the man again. He did indeed have a nose after all.

The man said, "I left my suitcase here and was hoping to pick it up."

Martin heard someone behind the desk saying that he'd have it right away.

Seconds later, a young man came out and started rolling the suitcase along the floor. Quickly, Martin pulled the eye up to his face. A little water sloshed from side to side and dripped onto his forehead.

The young man's nose vanished, and two words appeared: black male.

The eye zoomed in closer on the young man, scanning his body for weapons.

The following words scrolled past Martin's vision: no weapons.

Martin brought the glass down from his face. That was odd.

The young man looked nice enough. He wasn't sure why the eye had immediately scanned for a knife or a gun.

He felt his phone buzz. Setting the glass carefully on one leg and shielding the eye with his fingers, he pulled his phone out of his pocket and scanned his texts. There was one from his son and one from his ex-wife.

The ex-wife had written:

Glad to know you made it. Be safe there.

The son had written:

Proud of you, Dad.

They were both so kind to him, still, after everything. He'd been such a rotten grouch for so long, but he was still loved.

It depressed him to think of how awful he must've been to push good people away. If they had landed with someone better, maybe they would be happier.

Martin knew he wasn't ready to face the city. He went

back to the elevator, pushed the button and waited. He'd leave the eyeball in the room and get a proper breakfast before he did anything else.

He knew he wasn't dreaming.

He couldn't be sure as to whether or not he was hallucinating.

But he certainly wasn't dreaming.

Martin had eaten a mushroom omelet at a restaurant called *Gogol's Hot Eats*. He had eyed the full English breakfast but didn't think his stomach could handle that much grease. Maybe when he was younger, but not now.

No, he didn't want to go back to his hotel room with a stomach full of processed meats and have to deal with that thing in the glass. He'd ordered a tea and a coffee and drank both at the same time. He let the heat scald his teeth. He was trying to think.

The eye was real, and it seemed to overwrite whatever he saw with statistics and figures. He had no idea how he came into its possession. Perhaps it had been developed by military scientists or by an intelligence agency.

What was James Bond a part of? MI6. The eye was like something that Q would have shown James Bond before Bond got on a plane to go on a vodka-martini bender and blow up some exotic island.

Martin thought about the argument he'd had with his son over the Bond films. Martin's son had called Bond a 'colonial wet dream', whatever that meant. Martin had fired back, calling his son 'a thumb-sucking civvy'.

His son would never understand. He hadn't served his country. He'd just reaped the benefits.

And then they didn't talk for a month. It had been a month without little bright-eyed Sheree. That'd been tough.

When he'd finished both his coffee and his tea, Martin paid his bill and left for the hotel room. He decided that he wasn't quite ready to turn the eye over to authorities. He just needed a little more time to see what it could do, and then he would take it to the nearest police station.

123

He walked back to his hotel, went up the elevator, and opened the door to his room. The eye was trying to crawl out of the glass. He ran over to the thing, noticing its newly formed arms and legs, and tried to grab it before it could escape. But the eye had also formed a mouth with two rows of little fangs.

It dug its teeth into Martin's thumb.

Martin yelped and accidentally hurled the eye onto the bed.

He squeezed his bleeding hand and scanned the sheets, which were still a ruffled mess. He watched the movement, the little squiggling under the covers, and dove on top of the mattress hoping to catch the eye before it could escape.

Rolling around in the duvet, grasping for anything with shape or form, he saw the little figure moving on the carpet. He sat up, but the eye was running. Only then did he realise that he'd forgotten to close the door.

Throwing off the sheets, he followed the eye into the hallway where it was running to the elevator. The doors were about to close, but it rolled inside. When Martin got close enough, he pushed the button, but it was too late; the elevator was already moving.

He ran to the stairs and into the lobby, scanning for the eye, but he didn't have time to look. A hot burst of sound and light crashed in from the street. Glass shattered. A man near the front door was thrown five feet.

Martin stepped back behind the door and sat in the cool quiet of the stairwell. He just needed a half a second. He was going to pass out.

His brain was screaming at its skull.

His mouth was dry, and his joints ached.

He was too old for this nonsense.

So he had crawled back up the stairs and got under the covers. It was too much. He pulled his phone out of his pocket and texted his son and his ex-wife that he was OK. Then he pulled down the sheets and flicked on the news.

Despite the million little round cameras perched around the city, the hours of footage, the walls and walls of screens, no suspects had been identified. None of the talking heads on Martin's TV knew who left the explosive device so near his hotel in Southwark.

Martin's heart stuttered as he watched the narrative shift from the explosion to a series of smashed in windows in Piccadilly Circus. This act of vandalism appeared to be linked to the explosion and the rallies against climate change that were intended to be held over the weekend. Although nothing could be confirmed, it was reported that an extreme group, which went under the mysterious and threatening name of GACC, was responsible.

Despite his exhaustion, he smirked. The vandalism was being blamed on the group Martin had flown over to join, and they had only planned to hold peaceful protests. He didn't know any of the other members. Everyone went under a pseudonym.

Martin had gone under the name of Martian.

Even though he didn't know anyone's real name, he assumed from the message board that the members of GACC were people like him. They were elderly folks concerned with the extreme shifts in weather that they'd been watching and reading about.

They were average people who were worried about the type of world their grandchildren would inherit. The grandkids seemed to be pulling their own weight when it came to climate change. Why couldn't the grandparents?

A few days before Martin had left for London, he'd been surprised to find out that Sheree didn't put milk on her cereal. He asked her why and she told him it was because of her carbon footprint; it had something to do with reducing methane produced by cattle. Martin didn't fully understand it all, but he told the girl that she was a true wonder.

He was willing to sacrifice everything if it meant that little girl would have a brighter future.

He focused on the television for a few seconds and found himself chuckling despite his situation. Martin assumed that none of the talking heads on his TV actually knew what GACC stood for: Grandparents Against Climate Change.

The whole thing seemed laughable – that a group of eco-conscious, middle-class elderly folks were terrorizing London – but Martin knew that he needed to be cautious. A part of him wanted to stay in his room until his flight back to Canada, just to be safe.

He had come to England to meet people his own age and to stand up for a good cause, but he'd been thrown into a surreal conspiracy. Eventually, however, his stomach got the best of him, and he decided to go to the same place where he'd ordered the omelet.

An eerie purple calm rolled over the city as Martin walked past the site of the explosion, and he worried about the bomber. What if it had been someone from GACC?

He and the other group members had talked at length before they were to all gather in London. The protest had to be peaceful. Each and every person on the message board had agreed that if there was violence, those watching the protests on the news would turn against GACC. Furthermore, the authorities would have reasonable cause to shut GACC down and lock them up.

Martin saw *Gogol's Hot Eats*. The windows were boarded up, but the door was open. An arm popped out and a long finger pointed at Martin.

A familiar looking man in a suit came out, nodding. "Yes sir! Right away!" he said.

The man walked directly at Martin and grabbed him by the shirt.

Martin said, "Hello? How are you?"

The man didn't respond. He pulled Martin inside. Martin stumbled through the threshold. The tables were gone. There were four massive walls of screens, each one a recording of a different street.

"I'll have the omelet!" shouted Martin.

Why had he said that? He wasn't sure. He'd panicked and called out the first thing that came to mind.

"No omelet!" shouted the man who shoved him inside the kitchen.

Martin turned and saw a globe-shaped figure. Two arms

and two legs protruded from a perfectly round orb. It was about five feet tall now, the iris a deep, dark blue.

Martin said hello to the eye.

"You look hungry. I understand you like omelets," it said.

Martin nodded.

It stood quickly, shuffled to the fridge, and took out a tray of eggs. Then, it grabbed a bowl and begin cracking them. It whisked them and added cream. Flicking on the stovetop, it grabbed some butter and a frying pan.

Martin watched the thing dump the whisked eggs into the frying pan and cook.

"Are you a member of GACC?" asked the eye as it tilted the frying pan.

"I am," said Martin.

"What is GACC doing in London?" asked the eye.

"We were planning to hold a peaceful rally against the damage that human beings are inflicting on the earth," said Martin.

"Why London?" asked the eye, running a spatula around the egg and rolling it into a tube.

"London is an economic hub," said Martin. "Most of our members are living in the UK."

The eye finished cooking the omelet and slid it onto a plate. Walking over to Martin, it set the plate down with a fork and passed it to him.

Martin said thank you and began to fork the fluffy, buttery egg into his mouth.

"We have reason to believe that one of your people is responsible for the recent terrorist attack," said the eye. "We also know for a fact that your people have destroyed private property in the commercial district."

"That was never in the plans," said Martin, setting the fork down.

"We do not know about your plans. We only know what we have seen."

Martin swallowed whatever egg was left in his mouth.

The eye pulled the plate away from Martin and sat across from him.

"You are implicated in a terrorist attack," said the eye. "If you want to avoid incarceration, we suggest you help us."

Martin stared at the eye.

He knew he didn't have a choice.

GACC was meeting at The George Inn that night.

Groups of people were hunched around tables under the streetlights.

Their grey and white hair looked like an ashy snowfall.

About half of GACC had been arrested and were being detained. The few that remained were trying to understand what had happened.

Martin received little direction from the eye. He wasn't sure what he was supposed to do besides monitor the other members. So he walked up to one of the tables, said the codeword, and introduced himself by his pseudonym: Martian.

A grey-haired man with thick glasses nodded for him to sit. Martin knew this man only by his pseudonym: Claws.

"You're our alien Canadian?" asked Claws, pushing up his thick glasses.

"That's me," said Martin.

"Well, Mr. Canuck, we have been decimated," said a woman with short curly, steel coloured hair.

Martin knew her pseudonym was Tusk but nothing else.

She slid a beer over to him. "May as well drink up," she said.

"There's not much left to do," said Claws. "But sit back and have a pint of beer. All of this will not blow over. We've been had."

"What do you mean?" asked Martin.

Tusk plunked down her beer.

"The fuzz sent Agent Provocateurs to make us look like we are a pack of dirty criminals," she said and sighed. "Think about it. We wanted a peaceful protest. None of us wanted violence, and yet here we are dealing with a failed attempt to even begin because people who are supposedly associated with us destroyed public property before we could hit the streets."

"It's a chess game," said Claws. "And they've already got their checkmate."

"But why would the cops do that?" asked Martin.

Tusk shrugged and said, "I don't know, Martian. I'm just talking out of my backside. I'm guessing that they get heat from the big oil companies. They feel like they've got no choice."

Martin looked around and scanned the walls for CCTV cameras.

"I think it's MI6," said Martin.

"Why?" asked Claws.

"I don't know," said Martin. "I'm talking out of my backside, too."

"There's so much information floating around," said Tusk, "but we all know so little."

"We know they're watching us," said Martin quickly, holding the pint of beer over his mouth.

"Of course they are," said Claws. "But it's done. We can't even protest."

"They're not finished," whispered Martin. "They told me I had to come here."

Tusk nearly spit out her beer. "And you're telling us?" she asked.

"Who is they?" asked Claws.

Martin set his beer down on the table when he saw a round figure shift back from the edge of a building.

"I don't know," answered Martin, chugging the rest of his beer and standing, "but their leader is an overgrown eyeball."

Without saying goodbye, he walked towards the figure.

Turning the corner to the alleyway, he saw the round thing inside a beige jacket, two thin legs sticking out, and he called after it. "Wait!"

It turned. Martin saw grey hair underneath a blue, felted wool hat, and he was shocked to see that inside of that beige jacket was an eyeball.

"Good day, sir," came the voice of an elderly woman. "I see that you've been up to no good once again."

Before Martin could speak it was gone, down the alleyway and out another street.

He panicked.

This trip had been a mistake.

He hadn't even unzipped his darn suitcase.

He had started running after this new eye, but wasn't sure in what direction it had gone. Without the thing in sight, he still felt the need to move, to go unnoticed, to disappear for half a second. So he just kept jogging.

Jogging had always been a way for Martin to calm himself. Ever since his days in the forces, he'd felt the need to keep himself fit and ready. As he'd gotten older, he'd felt his knees giving way to mush whenever he jogged. But it felt good now. He felt young.

There were little parks, corners, and alleyways in which he felt a momentary sense of escape from all of the cameras and eyes following him.

But after fifteen minutes of jogging and sweating through a city that he didn't know at all, another feeling overcame him. He was lost in a place where 137 homicides had occurred in 2018. He kept jogging until he came to a busy street.

After a few attempts to wave down a cab, one finally stopped. He hopped into the back and told the cabbie the name of his hotel. Martin breathed deeply and wiped the sweat that was dripping down the side of one cheek. He would've asked the cabbie to drive all the way out to Heathrow and charge it to his credit card, but he'd left his passport at the hotel.

The cabbie just laughed and pointed out the window.

Martin looked over and saw that he had gotten into a cab directly outside of his hotel. He thanked the cabbie and stepped onto the sidewalk.

Immediately, he knew he had made a mistake. A circular orb of glass stuck to the wall seemed to follow his movements. He knew that whoever or whatever was on the other side of the camera was looking back at him.

He stepped into the hotel lobby and raced up the stairwell.

When he got to his door, he unlocked it, and slipped inside. The cool, clean dark of the room washed over him, and he felt for a moment that he could breathe. He closed his eyes and enjoyed the peace and the calm.

Then a lamp flicked on, and he saw a familiar looking man standing in the corner of his room.

"Have you ever been to Peru?" asked the man.

Martin didn't answer the question. Instead, he asked if he could get his passport.

The man shrugged his shoulders.

After Martin had grabbed his passport from his bag, the man escorted him down to the lobby and flagged a cab. When they were both in the back and the cab was moving, the man said, "I'm going to Peru tomorrow. Machu Picchu. You've never been there?"

Martin shook his head. His knees and his shins were throbbing. What had he been thinking, jogging like that?

"But you've heard about how they used to sacrifice the low born for the greater good?"

Martin didn't feel like engaging in this line of conversation. He smiled at the man. He knew where he had seen him before. Earlier that day in the lobby, he had seen this man picking up a suitcase.

However, he didn't want to show any sign of recognition.

He looked quickly away and said, "You know, I have heard about Machu Picchu. That's the place where the ruling class blocked themselves off from the rest of society. They watched their people from on high, at a distance. Their society completely collapsed."

The man sneered at Martin, then said to the driver, "We're here."

Martin and the man got out at *Gogol's Hot Eats*. They went in and Martin was shoved into a chair. He waited as two round figures came out of a back room. The eye was now accompanied by the other eye he'd just seen roughly an hour ago near The George Inn.

Introducing the newcomer as Iris, the eye said, "My dear lady has been telling us about your meeting outside of The

George Inn. Sounds like you went off-script."

"I would say very off-script, sir," said Iris. "In my humble opinion, he should be dealt with harshly. The moment I saw on the news that horrid GACC were blowing the capital up to smithereens, I hopped on the first train to keep my eye on the streets. And what did I see? I saw this fellow who sits before us conspiring with the very individuals who wish to do us wrong. I say lock them up. Lock them all up, Mr. Eye."

"Relax now, Iris," said Mr. Eye. "Martin will be dealt with. But I suggest we first give him a chance at redemption. Does redemption interest you, Martin?"

Martin had come to London for redemption. Of course it interested him.

He had spent his post-military life working on an oil rig off the coast of Newfoundland. He didn't understand global warming, but he had come to realize that it was going to make the world a worse place for his grandchildren.

He didn't feel like he'd done anything wrong by working on the oil rig. He'd provided for his family and lived a decent life. He hadn't really considered the damages caused by the oil and gas industry until one Christmas when he'd gotten into a heated argument with his son.

His son made an off-handed remark about global warming, and Martin had replied that he didn't believe it was real. There was a blizzard outside. How could the boy be going on about global warming when there was a snowstorm roaring just out the window?

Martin's son began a lecture about the differences between climate and weather. Martin felt insulted, talked down to. Martin had changed the boy's poopy diapers! Did he honestly think he was going to tell his father what's what?

The argument blew up.

Martin didn't even know how they'd begun screaming at one another.

He stormed out of the house. There wasn't anything he could've done while he was working on the rig. At the same time, he was learning now that that people needed to change if humanity was going to survive the drastic shifts in climate.

Joining GACC was a way to make things right again.

So when Mr. Eye asked him if he was interested in redemption, Martin had said yes. He just didn't reveal the specifics of that redemption.

"We are pleased to hear that you are interested in redemption, Martin," said Mr. Eye. "Bring out the bag, Iris."

Martin watched Iris leave the room and return with two halves of a singed suitcase.

"Here's what will happen, Martin. We need you to take this suitcase and plant it among prominent GACC members."

Martin immediately knew where he had last seen this suitcase. The man who'd been waiting for him in the hotel room, the same man who he'd seen in the hotel lobby the morning he'd arrived—he'd requested this bag from the front desk, and he'd wheeled it out onto the street before the explosion.

Martin had to conceal his rage when the full plot became clear to him.

"Why are you against GACC?" he asked.

"We are not against them in any way," said Mr. Eye. "We simply have orders to follow, and we follow them."

Martin nodded. "Tell me what you need me to do."

"Perhaps he is one of our people after all," said Iris.

It was late.

Martin didn't want to fall asleep.

He had the exploded suitcase and was awaiting further instructions.

The day had been so exhausting that the minute his head touched a pillow, he was in dreamland. He woke to the sound of the phone ringing. Rolling over, he grabbed the phone and pressed it to his ear.

It was Mr. Eye. "Wake up, Martin."

"I'm awake," he said. "How else would I be answering the phone?"

"We are not being literal, Martin. Now wake up."

Martin didn't understand what Mr. Eye meant, so he asked. "What do you want me to do next?"

133

"There are members of GACC who operate under the pseudonyms of Claws and Tusk," said Mr. Eye. "You sat with them during your indiscretion. We need you to take the suitcase to their home and leave the suitcase in their garage."

Martin asked for the address of their home.

When he finished on the phone with Mr. Eye, he showered and dressed. He took the exploded suitcase, which had been stuffed inside of a larger suitcase, and he left the hotel room.

Out on the street there was a cab waiting. He raised one hand to the driver, and when the cabbie nodded, Martin shoved the suitcase in the trunk and got in the back seat. He gave the driver the address to Claws and Tusk's house and felt the car pulling him along.

He remembered that he hadn't checked his cellphone in a little while. He opened it up and saw that his son and his ex-wife had been texting him while he'd been asleep. He couldn't think of how to write back, so he just stuffed his phone back in his pocket and looked at the cabbie.

"On second thought," said Martin, "just take me to the nearest police station."

The driver nodded, no shift in his expression.

A few minutes later they pulled to the curb. Before Martin could reach his wallet, the driver had come around to the side of the door and opened it.

"You'll need to come inside with me," he said, pulling off his beard.

"I thought you were going to Peru," said Martin.

"My trip was cancelled," said the man.

Martin realized that he was outside of *Gogol's Hot Eats* once again. The man guided him in, and when Martin walked through the door, he felt a different energy in the room. A chair was positioned before a camera.

The man patted Martin on the back. "I hope you can relax, Martin," he said. "I'm going to have to ask you a few questions."

Martin sat in the chair before the camera. The rows of screens wheeled away, revealing a small audience, a hundred eyes staring.

The man sat behind the camera. "Have you heard of Candid Camera?" he asked.

"I have," Martin said. "It's where somebody has a trick played on them, and the whole thing is being recorded."

The man laughed. "That's right. Well, I'm your host, Charles Salt."

He reached out and shook Martin's hand.

"Nice to meet you," said Martin.

"You are on Britain's newest reality TV show in which we put people in extreme situations and see if they do the right thing."

Martin laughed. "Did I do the right thing?" he asked.

Charles Salt crossed his legs. "Well," he said, "Let's hear about it from your point of view. What do you think? Tell us how and why you joined Grandparents Against Climate Change, more commonly referred to as GACC, for any audience members who have never heard of them. And we're just recording this, Martin. We're not live, so feel free to stop and correct yourself at any time."

Martin couldn't believe that all of this was part of some elaborate TV show. Claws and Tusk must've only been actors. He thought about his flight back to Canada, which was leaving that night. It was looking like he'd miss it, but he didn't care if he was going to be a celebrity in the UK.

With the heat of the lights blaring down on him, Martin launched into the story of how he had worked most of his life on an oil rig only to realize in his old age that he wanted to give something back, if only for the sake of his granddaughter.

Charles Salt asked him how he'd gotten into contact with GACC.

Martin talked about how he was disappointed that GACC was only part of a reality TV show because he believed that if the elderly banded together over the right causes, they could be an important force for good in the world.

When the interview was over, Charles Salt reached out and shook Martin's hand once again.

"I think we have everything we need," he said, and

snapped a pair of handcuffs around Martin's wrists.

Martin was led out of the makeshift studio as the audience members started to leave the building.

Charles Salt shoved him through a door.

Mr. Eye and Iris were both waiting on the other side.

"You ought to be ashamed of yourself," Iris said. "Coming from the colonies, you'd think you would have some semblance of respect." She shook her head. "Well, I have no time for this tomfoolery. I shall be heading back to the countryside and to my garden."

Iris left the room, tsk-tsking Martin as she went.

"It was all a hoax?" asked Martin. "The TV show?"

"We will need to escort you to a facility," Mr. Eye said. "Your cooperation or lack thereof in this incident has been noted. Your family in Canada will be informed of your incarceration."

Martin looked down at his handcuffs. "I didn't do anything wrong," he said.

"Guilt by association," said Mr. Eye.

"GACC didn't do anything wrong," said Martin.

Charles Salt turned Martin around and escorted him from the room.

Martin was shoved into an alleyway and escorted to a black car. Before he got in, however, he saw five round figures dressed in black cloaks.

"God sees everything!" they chanted. "The state sees nothing! God sees everything! The state sees nothing! God sees everything! The state sees nothing!"

Martin saw an arm fling out from one of the cloaks and a flaming bottle soared at the black car. The explosion rocked Martin backwards into the brick wall, squishing Charles Salt behind him.

The five figures hurled Molotovs at the car. The explosion burst back their cloaks. Martin saw that each one was a giant eyeball with a thick wooden cross dangling between its legs.

Martin felt inside Charles Salt's pockets, taking out the keys and undoing the handcuffs. Salt seemed to be waking up as Martin turned to run, so he waved down a cab and hopped in.

He sat, looking out the window, stunned by everything he'd seen. He'd only been in London for two days, and he'd barely survived.

Martin realized that he wouldn't be able to make it through the airport security with its various cameras and checkpoints. He asked the driver to pull over to the side of the road. He paid and got out.

He was trapped in London until he dealt with Mr. Eye.

Martin walked into a Tesco.

He paid in cash.

He bought everything he needed to make a bomb.

He locked himself inside a public bathroom, and he struggled to remember exactly how to create the explosive device. An old army buddy had taught him how to do it while they were on a hunting trip. They had built two bombs and tried to blow up a bear that had stolen a package of their hotdogs. They ended up creating a massive scorched hole in a clearing and scaring all the animals away.

When Martin finished making the explosive device, he put it back in a plastic bag and went looking for *Gogol's Hot Eats*. He sent a quick text to his son:

Love ya. Tell Sheree I ate cereal with water. LOL!

The sidewalks outside *Gogol's Hot Eats* were scorched. Police tape was around the singed car. There was a single police officer standing nearby with his arms crossed. He didn't look in Martin's direction.

Martin walked inside. No one was there. He called out, and he saw Mr. Eye appear from behind a door. The thing waddled over to him, its pupil scanning him up and down.

"Why did you come back?" Mr. Eye asked.

"I knew I wouldn't be able to get out of the airport," said Martin.

"Unless you dealt with us," said Mr. Eye, finishing Martin's thought.

Martin didn't reply. He watched Mr. Eye glance at the bag in his hand.

"You must understand," said Mr. Eye, "that without us, everything devolves into chaos. All of those nice parks suddenly become sites for potential crimes. Those subways that people find so convenient end up being places where pregnant women get attacked. Wherever there is a steady and consistent presence of surveillance, muggings decrease, violent crime decreases."

"But who's watching you?" asked Martin.

"There are systems in place," Mr. Eye replied.

Martin started to reply, but Mr. Eye pushed him and ran outside. Martin chased after, but the minute he stepped out, he crashed into someone. As they were getting up from the sidewalk, this person picked up Martin's bag and unintentionally glanced inside.

Having worked for five years on the bomb squad for the London Police Department, he immediately recognized the object in the bag as an explosive device.

Martin saw the change of expression on the man's face. He said, "I can explain."

"Put your hands up, sir," the man ordered.

"But wait you just have to hear me out," said Martin.

The man waved over the police officer who had been standing nearby.

"You'll have to explain to the proper authorities," said the man.

Martin sighed and handed over the bomb. He had put up a good fight, but he accepted defeat. In that moment, the order of the universe had become disturbingly clear, and Martin knew that he was living in a farce.

Tom Halford lives in beautiful Corner Brook, Newfoundland, Canada. He and his wife, Melissa, work at Grenfell Campus Memorial University of Newfoundland. They have two amazing, hilarious kids who enjoy Pokemon and superheroes.

Tom holds a doctorate in English Language and Literature, and he studies representation of surveillance. His first novel is titled Deli Meat, and he hopes to finish another novel before too long. You can follow him on Twitter: @tomhalfordnovel

Follow Tom's Blog: **www.tomhalfordblog.wordpress.com**

Ghosts of Whitechapel

Denise Bloom

Authors Note

Emma Elizabeth Smith was attacked in April 1888 and died the following day from her injuries. Her murder was not attributed to the notorious serial killer Jack the Ripper. His reign of terror was thought to have started on the 31st August 1888 with the murder of Mary Ann Nichols.

However, some ripperologists suggest that Emma Smith could have been his first victim. This story is fictional.

Old Montague Street.
Whitechapel 1888.

The workhouse was as dark on the inside as the outside. The sorrowful throng that paced the tiled corridors, were those without hope. They had claimed sanctuary in its regimented wards because they were unable to earn a crust in the outer world. The old, the infirm and those without full mental capacity spent their days picking oakum until their fingers bled. They were guaranteed three meals a day. However, it was not fare that was on the table of the gentry. Breakfast consisted of a slice of bread with dripping. Lunch time saw a watery soup of vegetables and in the evening a stew or potatoes with maybe a portion of cheese or a scrap of meat.

In 1888 there was a record of eight hundred and fifty people: six hundred women and children and two hundred and fifty men. The infirmary ward was mixed, but otherwise families were separated, with women and children in one section and males in the other.

The custodians were headed by the matron, Mrs. Gaskill. She ruled the establishment with an iron fist. There was a budget for each person, and as the matron oversaw the bookkeeping, she skimmed an amount every month. She was able to do this by cutting the food rations to their minimum. The money was meant for her retirement in Margate. Mrs. Gaskill believed people of a certain class and culture needed to be hungry; it encouraged hard work. She was supported in her role by Robert Mann and James Hatfield who worked in the mortuary. There were frequent deaths in the workhouse, mostly due to the poor diet and the illnesses that were rife in that part of London. The River Thames was an open sewer, with human waste spilling into it, along with the by-products of the many industries that had sprung up along its banks as the industrial revolution steamed its way through the century.

***

Robert Mann had arrived at the workhouse with his parents when he was twelve years old. At the age of sixteen, he joined the navy and sailed the seas for four years. On arriving back in London, he jumped ship and got lost in Whitechapel. He met James Hatfield in the Ten Bells tavern. James had survived two wives and was drowning his sorrows in the best porter. They made an unlikely couple – James being tall and skinny and Robert short and rotund – but they had a similar outlook on society. They both thought they had been dealt a poor hand in life and that they deserved a lot better.

Silas Jackson was one of their drinking friends. He was a

quack doctor living on Brick Lane. One night, they were sitting at their corner table in the snug, warming their hands on the fire that burnt brightly in the grate.

"Robert, James, I am so pleased that you are here. I have a proposition for you," Silas said.

The two men were all ears. A proposition sounded like they were about to line their threadbare pockets.

"I have a very good friend, a Mrs. Gaskill, who is the matron at the workhouse in Old Montague Street. She is in need of two trustworthy men who would suit as assistants in the mortuary, which is situated at the rear of the workhouse."

The two men looked at each other. They had not planned to work in a proper job.

"I have told her that I knew of two men who had been in the navy and who were looking for honest employment."

They were both surprised that Silas had then thought of them.

"We don't have to live in the workhouse, do we?" Robert was not keen on a job where he had to be in for eight o'clock and lights out by nine.

"No, that's the good thing. There are two rooms that could be used as your own in the mortuary itself." Silas sat back and waited for the response.

"That sounds like a deal to me James." The two friends looked at each other, then shook hands.

Silas wrote the name of the matron and a short note for the men to take with them.

***

Mrs. Gaskill looked the two men in front of her up and down. She liked that their boots were clean. They seemed to have a little intelligence about them, but not too much. They had to know their place.

"Well, Mr. Jackson says that you have been in the navy."

Robert nodded. James stared at the floor.

"Good. I will show you the premises. Follow me!" She strode ahead, with Robert and James following on her heels.

"The doctor comes most days to visit the infirmary and to pronounce deaths. Unfortunately, there are quite a few due to the poor souls we deal with. Bodies arrive here at all hours of the day and night. Vagrants who are found in doorways, dead from the cold, have to be picked up. The police also bring prisoners who have passed away in custody. You will then have to contact a doctor whose name is on the list behind the door to come and certify death. I am too busy to have my sleep disrupted through the night, so I need people who are dependable and trustworthy. Any slight question of this and you will be thrown out. Are we clear?"

Both men nodded, and Mrs. Gaskill was content that they would not challenge her authority.

***

Robert was in awe; this woman had the strength lacking in many a man. She was straightforward, and he knew she had a secret.

They were taken to a ramshackle building that was situated at the rear of the workhouse. The smell hit them as she opened the oak door. Death has a special aroma, and it had penetrated the very fabric of the building. Large black flies buzzed around them, hoping to take a bite from the living. The mortuary room housed two wooden gurneys complete with bodies covered by sheeting.

James felt his stomach heave but managed to keep his porter down.

The building had a number of rooms. Two were to be their bedrooms complete with straw mattresses. There was a basic kitchen with a grate where they could boil a kettle. The rooms were cleaner than the lodgings they had at Mrs. Parkinson's. It had been a good move, even if they had to share it with the dead.

Mrs. Gaskill left them with a great bunch of brass keys and told them that they were able to take their meals in the kitchen. They also received a ration of tea, milk and bread. A covered cart in the yard was used to transport dead bodies, and the workhouse kept a piebald horse in the stable, munching hay as they passed. Mrs. Gaskill said they could use the horse and cart to collect their meagre belongings from their lodging house.

Robert looked at himself in the window of the outfitters. Each man had been supplied with a custodian's uniform: good trousers, waistcoats and topcoats. He smoothed down the jacket, feeling like a real gent. He may have been short of money, but he had a roof over his head and regular food.

That evening, they went to the Ten Bells and met up with Silas.

"Well, my friends you seem to be doing well for yourselves."

Robert had bought an extra drink for Silas. "We are very happy, Silas, very happy. Mrs. Gaskill is a good matron, and our accommodation is comfortable. However, the food at the workhouse is wanting. Guess we need to find a little more employment elsewhere so we can feed ourselves properly."

They all knew about the delights of workhouse gruel.

"There is another way you can earn a shilling or two," Silas said.

Robert and James leant forward to catch every word.

"I know a professor who lives not too far from here. He needs bodies for dissection. He is working on ways to cure many illnesses, but it is exceedingly difficult to acquire fresh cadavers." Silas waited for the reaction of his two friends. Their faces did not change.

Robert was the first to speak. "Silas, I am sure that I speak for James as well as myself that we are grateful that you have brought this business to our door. Most of our departed are buried in paupers' graves, or on the odd occasion taken to the London hospital for the new doctors to practise on. Why does the professor not apply for a body in the usual way?"

Silas smiled. "Because the work that he is doing is secret." He tapped the side of his nose. "The money is very good if you can promise a weekly supply."

James and Robert leant towards each other and whispered. Finally, Robert said, "We don't see a problem there. Have you the address?"

The deal was done, and the mortuary assistants were happy they had another income. Soon, they already had the first body that could be redirected from St Mary's churchyard to Wilton Street. Many others followed.

A year later, Robert Mann and James Hatfield had established themselves as trustworthy custodians of the mortuary. The coroners and doctors who used the premises saw the odd couple as men who were able to take orders and perform autopsies without turning a hair.

The professor who was accepting bodies for his research refused to take any cadaver that had been dissected, so they were buried in the usual manner.

They had fallen into a routine. In the workhouse, the matron would inform them when an inmate was unlikely to survive the night. On a few occasions, they had helped the odd inmate along their way when visiting the infirmary ward if they were short of their weekly number. Those in the sick ward who were taking their final breaths lived their last moments in terror.

Robert and James had a very profitable business and spent their money throughout the east end of London. Most people recognised the two as they ate in the pie shops and drank in most of the local taverns.

One working day, the bell rang above the mortuary door. A young woman, Mrs. Turner, inquired about a body that had been brought in from the sugar factory. The deceased had fallen from the roof and broken his neck. What was surprising for Robert was that the woman, although dressed in a plain stuff skirt and threadbare jacket, spoke as though she should be wearing silk and bows. Her manners were those of a true lady. He showed her the body on the wooden gurney. She obviously loved her husband as she was heartbroken but tried to keep her feelings under control. Robert admired the strength she had. Trying to use his best manners, Robert directed Mrs. Turner to Marlow & Marlow, the local funeral directors they used. There was an agreement that Robert would advise any relative of the deceased to use Marlow & Marlow in return for a small commission. This woman, although poor, was going to give her husband a decent burial.

Over the next couple of years, Robert and James often came across Mrs. Turner. Eventually, Robert introduced himself when seeing her in one of the local taverns.

"Mrs. Turner, good evening. I'm Mr. Mann, custodian at Old Montague Street." She recognised him he was sure.

"Good evening, sir. I remember." Then she turned towards her friends, clearly not intending to take part in further discussion.

He returned to his glass of porter.

"You are foolish, Robert. She ain't going to have owt to do with you.".

"Surely every woman wishes to have a man, James?" Robert knew his friend had some bad experiences with women. "London Town is a bad place; women need protection."

"That lot need a man to line their pockets." He sneered. Women were aplenty in the taverns and available for a few pennies, but you never knew what you would get from them. He did not mean just sexual diseases but cholera, typhoid and tuberculosis. Disease was rife in the area due to the polluted water and poor diet of the masses.

Then, Robert began to see Mrs. Turner with another man. Patrick Smith was little more than a lout. He dressed well for the area, but he dealt with the scum of society, stealing and dealing in smuggled goods. Robert couldn't understand why the woman would choose this blaggard over him. Maybe he didn't present himself as the catch he was.

One evening, he noticed she now called herself Mrs. Smith, although Robert doubted that she had married the oaf. He was sure that Smith was married to another woman near Spitalfields Market. Mrs. Smith sat in the corner of the Ten Bells nursing a glass of gin, whilst her beloved stood chatting with a whore at the bar.

Mrs. Smith had a bruise to her eye and a cut lip. Robert

147

felt a little sad at the way the woman had spiralled downwards; she was now part of the Whitechapel underclass. He knew James thought it was what he expected – women drained the life out of men. If you weren't lining their pockets with silver, they turned into old crones. They had discussed this before, but Robert had never been married; he had not experienced the ways of women.

Three months later, Robert read in the newspaper that Smith had been locked up for robbery and gone down for twenty-five years. Good enough for me, thought Robert. *I might try my hand with the woman.*

She would be about town and if she was down on her luck, then he, Robert Mann, could be her saviour. A man with prospects was more desirable than having to sell your body on the street.

Mrs. Smith was out in the Britannia one night with the whore that Patrick Smith had kept. But she still turned her back on his advances, and he did not take it well.

Who the hell does she think she is?

James told him he was a fool. If he wanted a tiff, there was a multitude of whores for the taking at two pennies each. But what Robert really wanted was to increase his status. Mrs. Smith would be someone who could open more doors for him. He would be accepted into a different circle.

Society was cruel in the Victorian age. It was the age of the family, and family commanded respect. Over the following weeks, he tried to buy Mrs. Smith a drink. He could tell she had the need for it now, but she still would not have anything to do with him. More and more, he resented her refusal of friendship.

Robert remembered the time she had first come to the mortuary; she had been young and fresh, like a rose ready to be picked. He looked at her now – a wreck of a woman. The drink had turned her complexion grey, she had missing teeth and clothes that were threadbare. And after all that she still wouldn't look at him, the bitch. James was right. He knew about women. Robert should have listened to him.

The young girl that Mrs. Smith was with went with a customer into the yard at the back of the tavern. James and Robert stood in the dark shadows. Robert was disappointed that it wasn't her; he was determined to get his revenge. The girl lifted her skirts. They heard the moaning and groaning from the lad, and a gasp when he had reached his climax.

She giggled. "Thank you, kind sir. Look for me next time; you will always have a smile from Kate."

The boy stumbled from the yard. Robert slipped silently from his hiding place with James at his elbow. Kate didn't have a chance. Robert hit her with a silver-topped driving stick. There was a sharp intake of breath from her, then she collapsed to the floor.

James bent over and slit her throat, the blood spurting onto the flagstones.

Robert was breathing quickly, his saliva dripping onto Kate.

James took the florin she still had in her hand. They looked around hoping they had not been seen, then rapidly went to the horse and cart. Kate was left in a crumpled heap on the cold ground.

After reaching the mortuary, they both changed out of their blood-stained shirts. Not that anyone would think it unusual; it was the business they were in.

The next day, Robert took the garments into the laundry for washing. As he expected, the women were not asking any questions. Robert still wished that the girl in the back yard had been Mrs. Smith. It was disappointment he felt; he would have his revenge he was sure. That woman used people; he could see it was no wonder that Patrick Smith had beaten her.

Robert was in a good mood most of the day. He had enjoyed the thrill of stalking their prey and the slicing of the throat, it had brought back good memories of his childhood. He'd worked on a farm, butchering animals from being a small boy.

It was the third of April 1888. Robert and James went to the Blind Dog for a glass or two of ale after they had eaten a fine supper of meat and potatoes. They watched a group of women that sat in front of the burning logs in the grate. The women were cackling like a coven of witches, all well-oiled with gin. Several sailors on shore leave with full purses were buying them drinks. The door opened and Mrs. Smith found a seat next to her friends around the grate. She was looking a little better, with her hair combed and a little rouge to her cheeks.

Robert Mann turned so his back was to the bar. He watched her as she smiled to the sailors.

"After all I have said, James, she is still a grand woman."

James Hatfield turned to see who Robert was looking at. He raised his eyes to the ceiling. "No point looking; she ain't going to have owt to do with you." He turned back to finish his drink, shaking his head.

"The way she speaks, she is like a lady."

"She's a tuppenny whore, quick to take your money but slow to open her thighs."

When James ordered more drinks, Robert went over to the table to greet Mrs. Smith.

"Good evening, Mrs. Smith. It is wonderful to meet you on this pleasant evening."

"Good evening, sir," she said, squirming in her seat.

"Please allow me to buy you a gin or a glass of porter?"

"Thank you, no, sir."

Her friends were making crude remarks which Robert didn't find humorous. He could tell she really wanted to accept the drink; she was at that time of life when drink had taken her soul. So he asked again, and she relented. He bought her a glass of porter with a small gin chaser. It didn't take long for her to empty her glasses and for Robert to replenish them. He thought his luck was in, though she could take her drink, there was no doubt about that.

"May I take you to your lodgings, Mrs. Smith?"

She shook her head. "No, sir. I am capable of walking home myself." She did not even look at him.

"You have emptied my pockets, madam." Robert couldn't understand this woman. She was sitting with a bunch of whores. Her clothes were torn and threadbare, her boots were well worn. Yet she still rejected him.

"You have emptied your pockets freely, sir."

There was another cackle from the coven. He turned on his heel and picked up his cane from the bar. James slung his ale down and joined him on leaving the tavern.

"She is the devil himself, James."

His friend didn't say anything. Robert was about to explode. They went to the cart and Robert took the reins. He snapped the leather and the horse jolted to a start.

"She needs to be taught a lesson, Robert. We can't have women like that making a fool of us. We are respected men in the workhouse. We are not inmates."

Robert nodded. His friend was right. "I agree. No woman is going to make a fool out of me, James. What do you say?"

The tall skinny body of James Hatfield turned towards him. He resembled a dead body, thought Robert, with his sunken cheeks and now showing teeth like gravestones. "She does indeed."

The fog swallowed the cart as they waited on the corner of Brick Lane.

***

Emma Smith hoped that the two men had returned to the mortuary. They would have been the last people she wanted to meet on a dark night. She said her goodnights to the company she had been in. Her bed was calling, and she was happy to be going back to her lodgings. Some of the women she had drunk with would be sleeping in a doorway that night.

The night was cool. A fog was swirling from the river. She was going to be late back at the lodging house and would have to knock for Tilly to let her in. Tonight felt strange. Whitechapel was usually busy. The weather must have encouraged people to stay indoors.

Emma had consumed an enormous amount of liquor and had to steady herself on a couple of occasions, holding onto the walls of buildings. She reached the corner of Brick Lane and Osborn Street when she heard a horse and cart plodding across the cobbles. As it passed, she saw two passengers, swaddled in thick coats, hunched over. Then they disappeared into the swirling fog. A cough sounded ahead of her, but she couldn't see anyone. Staggering on the flagstones, she noticed the outline of the same cart before her. The horse snorted as it struck its shoes on the ground. Emma wondered where the occupants could have gone when, from a shop doorway, a dark figure jumped out and swiftly put a sack over her head. It must have had coal in it at some time, as she could smell and taste the dust. She screamed as loud as she could, but a hand was planted tightly across her mouth. Her legs thrashed to try and escape the hands that were holding her. Then she realised that there was more than one person as another pair of hands grabbed her legs. She was now lying on her back.

A voice whispered into her ear, "Free with everything, you tart."

Fear gripped her and she struggled again, but she was held fast. Hands explored her body, grabbing at her breast and reaching under her petticoats.

"Hand me my driving stick," the voice snarled.

Her petticoats were thrown over her head, and the cold air ran across her belly. Then a hard object was thrust inside her – the driving stick! She let out one scream, then descended into a dark world of nightmares.

When she regained consciousness, she still had the coal sack over her head and pulled it off. The pain in her groin stabbed her as a stiletto blade had done. Emma knelt and pulled her skirt down, feeling the blood flowing down her legs. She had to get back home. She could not die in the street.

Emma half walked half crawled back to her lodging house. Managing to pull herself up to reach the window, she rapped with all her might to awaken Tilly. The young girl looked out and could see that she was hurt. Mrs. Russel, the deputy matron, opened the door ready to scold Emma but, finding her in such deep distress, helped to her bed. Within a minute the sheets were covered with blood.

"Who has done this to you, Emma?"

She couldn't speak at first, then a tiny voice said, "Men, men."

"Oh Lord, save us; we must take her to the hospital."

Mrs. Russel and Tilly helped Emma to The London Hospital in Whitechapel where she was taken to a ward and made comfortable. Tilly returned to the lodgings, but Mrs. Russel stayed with Emma, holding her hand. The doctors said that the patient had been attacked and that a blunt object had punctured her peritoneum. There was little hope for her.

Emma Smith died at 8.45am on the fourth of April 1888. The body was taken to the workhouse mortuary on Old Montague Street, Whitechapel.

At the coroner's court, the two mortuary assistants, who had taken part of the post-mortem, sat beside each other.

James Hatfield leant over to Robert Mann and whispered, "She got what she deserved."

Satisfied, Robert Mann nodded. "They all deserve it. Dirty whores, the lot of them."

Denise Bloom was born and brought up in Bradford West Yorkshire and now lives in the South West of France. She has an Honours Degree in Social Sciences. Always interested in writing she wrote short stories within a creative writing group.

After encouragement from others she has gone on to publish her book, The Ladies of Whitechapel – covering four stories with a common thread. Each story is the life of a woman that lived in 1888.

When not writing Denise enjoys reading, usually history. Painting and volunteers for a cancer support charity.

Follow Denise on Twitter: **www.twitter.com/DLBloom_16**

Forty-Three

Harper Channing

I leave for you, reader, this, my own final and candid expression of that dear friend, Mr. Jacob Finlay, born to a penniless unfortunate, not a stone's throw from St. Mary le Bow, on the morning of the very same day as the great Coronation. It had been Jacob's true and trusted belief that illusion should play no lesser part in the ebb and flow of his life than that of Queen Victoria's own, illusion so detailed a blueprint for the machinery of love and devotion.

I know not how Jacob ascended from the gutters. Perhaps it was his first great invention of illusion, for he must surely have possessed neither the schooling nor the unwavering dedication necessary to legitimately become apprenticed to Mr. John Burnet of Bow, who had followed his grandfather, the late, great and respected clockwork maker, Mr. Thomas Burnet of Bow, into the same dedicated and precise craft. But that was the place Jacob did, indeed, find himself.

We may forget that the very thing we take to our measurement of the world was once crafted for our singular enjoyment. I tell you that this was the age in which the timepiece had become popular. It was in this age, in this space of the seventy-four years between grandfather and grandson, that the craft of horology itself would bear witness to noticeable change. At the close of those years, it is true that each small town in England had the means to manufacture a device for timekeeping so inexpensive of value that a perfect copy of it would rest upon the mantelpiece of every other house there. And what is more is that in the pockets and on the wrists of every suitable gentleman in London would once rest a watch that was made up of two-hundred-and-three pieces. The number was standard for many years, for watches of the wrist had not evolved with swift pace. At the close of the Burnets' seventy-four years, that watch was made up of fifty-nine pieces. Its revolutionary design was that of a Mr. George Redkop of Upminster, who named it the 'Proletariat'. He asked not a penny more than nine shillings for it.

If it were not for the romantically-aligned artisan skill and keen inventiveness of the craftsman, then the world may not have imagined models of timekeeping that were both simpler and more attractive, and that would appeal less so to the masses, but more to the refined of society.

And so it was that, at the age of twenty-four years, Jacob had, by all accounts, become skilled in over three dozen horological practices, all of which are certainly too technical for a layperson such as I to recount. It is fortunate, then, that the notes and correspondence belonging to young Jacob, nearly a shelfful in fact, which I have recently come into possession of, lead me to believe that he was other than his history would have us believe. I understand, you see, that it would be commonplace to expect such skill of which I speak, of a watchmaker with a good twenty-five or thirty years' experience behind them. If that were not indication enough of illusion, a further discovery, on my part, which emerged from those acquired papers, was that, by his twenty-sixth year, Jacob wrote, with great fluency, in the French language.

I am of a certain mind that some would not be as struck with Jacob's knowledge of French as I was. Horology, you see, is a practice whose greatest masters and most respected associations are Francophone by nature, the learnings written and passed down in that same tongue. But that the vast history of a brotherhood should be told in one language does not mean each brother should know it word for word. You see, I myself was trained in London as a Doctor of Medicine, and practised, for much of my life, in the north of England. One would be assured to say that I barely managed more than a glance at Latin, my profession's learned mother tongue, in spite of my formative years at grammar school. I would not say, with the greatest wish in the world, that I could endeavour to correspond lucidly, my 'amats', and 'amants' quite all over the place.

I do, as it happens, believe that I know the wherefores of how it came to be that Jacob moved from one social standing to another – to acquire fluency in the French language, to engage in a skilled career. But I shall save this for another time.

There are occasions where I believe it may have been the happenings of one night that changed the course of Jacob's life. I realise that I believe this to be a universal truth. Are we not all so often swayed in our beliefs by a singularly inconsequential matter, thereafter to ponder to the point of personal illumination? And so it was, his papers tell, that he found himself on one of many dozens of errands, requested of him by his employer, to deliver the object of a commission of work: a pocket watch of otherwise rather normal standing. The patron had requested that they meet outside the theatre, in the east of London, wherein he would enjoy a Wednesday night performance.

I myself remember that The Pavilion was grand, certainly. And it was grand not only by the standards of Whitechapel, lest we not remember how far that community has risen and fallen in recent years, but by the standards of the city entire. If memory serves, the theatre held over two-thousand without a strain. I seem to recall the enjoyment of seeing a performance by Lilian Ryland there, enjoyment no less from the sound of her beautiful and melancholy voice, than from the atmosphere of the room. The Pavilion was for the very reason of its high regard that men and women such as those who commission pocket watches would gather in a part of London that otherwise they would not desire to set foot in.

For Jacob, the whereabouts bore no reason for fright. The east of London was his home, and a home is not to be analysed and picked apart. It is to be lived in. His notes do not deliver to us, as it happens, a fully rounded impression of the theatre itself, or of the patron, or of the watch to which I refer. I believe any nervous terror in Jacob may have come from the event in question – that performance. In mind of him, as I am, as an older gentleman, I might budge a guess to presume that there was as much chance his youthful self should have chosen to frequent such parlours of entertainment as much as to have debated at the Zoological Society of London.

No, his account of it is that the gentleman accepted delivery of the timepiece at the theatre, and, as a gesture of kindness, offered Jacob one ticket for that evening. The performance was not a theatrical one, nor was it musical. For those I think that my friend could have borne the ninety minutes out, his mind otherwise occupied by anything other than the drone of theatrics. Instead, I should explain that the Grangecroft Brothers, who indeed were brothers, though not called Grangecroft at birth, were the named act. You may know that the Spiritualist movement was in its ascendency at this time, at least as far as I recall, in the United States of America. The brothers represented the most engaging performance that the movement had to offer. I rather think that they must have chosen their shared name in order to seek acclaim not only from their own countrymen and women, but indeed also to seek it from those in countries where the name Grangecroft might appear somewhat lofty. This would not be the matter of their only illusion.

In spite of his lack of detail thus far, on this matter my friend Jacob is clear. The performance was introduced with great enthusiasm and pomp by a former Restoration Movement Minister, and now longtime acolyte of Spiritualism, one Dr. F. L. Hannering. He assured to the auditorium that the brothers worked without any degree of trickery, but instead by spirit power.

With that the lights fell entirely and, for the briefest of

moments, were held down. I daresay that in a theatre of this type for such a happening to have taken place at the commencement of a performance must have elicited from the room a good deal of murmur. We must be certain that this was, indeed, the intended outcome. Seemingly, the lights lifted with no great pace and now, upon the apron of the stage where the doctor had stood, was an otherwise plain wooden box – as tall as halfway up the front curtain, and as wide again. Two moderately large holes, each the shape of a square, had been cut into the front panel of the box, and those patrons seated in the front rows were very likely to have been able to catch a glimpse through them of the very things inside. All others would also see the same moments later.

With some force, the panel opened. Inside this compartment, on either side, sat a Grangecroft brother, their legs tied with large ropes to pegs attached to the wooden seats beneath them, their faces motionless. Silence. In between the brothers, in a space of roughly the same as that which they each occupied, sat a string guitar, and on a small table to its right was a collection of handbells and a trumpet. A violin hung just above them, its bow neatly placed by the side and, on the floor below the violin sat three small drums, their tensioners of rope and leather, the kind one might witness being banged at a ceremonial gathering.

Dr. Hannering walked once more onto the stage, his approach eliciting a carefully poised utterance of applause. Perhaps the patrons gathered that night wondered what was inside the white paper bag which he carried with him then. He declared that, in the presence of God, what the auditorium was about to witness was indeed true, and turned to the bow. The brothers held out their empty hands to the gaze of the audience. From the bag, Dr. Hannering poured a powdery substance into the palms of the first brother and then into those of the second, a puff of white dust lifting into the air above each set of hands as the substance settled. He told the audience that talcum powder would be the brothers' judge.

Well, I shall not hold on this any longer, reader, for I believe you know the outcome. It was such that Jacob and everyone seated there witnessed the panel close tight and, following a dramatic pause, I might presume, one brother requested that the spirits allow themselves to be known, at which occasion the strings of the guitar sounded a singular and clear note, and this was followed by a chord of repeated notes. His brother then asked for certain confirmation of the spirit's being. There was no rhythmic tick to the drum's response. It was as if a child had been given carefree opportunity to make music. A pause, then, and what followed was the broken, scattered toots from the trumpet. This upset the auditorium most of all. How might the brothers have engaged themselves with this instrument when all the while, as indeed it had been the case, they could be seen, seated motionless, through the windows at the front of the box?

Jacob describes, then, a whirligig of controlled hysteria, which moved, with gradual but continued pace, from the front of the auditorium to his own seat there, at the very top of the house. A good number of those that had paid a pretty package were now on their feet, one keen eye in the direction of the exit door. Those behind them observed as Dr. Hannering returned to the stage to request calm. Patrons from the middle seats had now vacated them, wanting nothing whatsoever to do with the events in front. The panel of the box opened once more, revealing the instruments in their original and untouched positions. Those at the back of the house, just on the verge of moving their sedentary position watched as Dr. Hannering untied the ropes that had bound the two men's feet.

Now surrounded by frenzy, Jacob rose. His notes say that he felt as if he was the only person in the theatre that night who witnessed brothers Oscar Lewis and Earl Herman Grangecroft cup their hands forward and pour out onto the floor in front of them the undisturbed mound of white powder that had been given to them earlier.

Jacob remained quite fixed to the spot. He saw something else, a second happening on the stage, that no other soul in that theatre noted – indeed, the brothers intended for no-one ever to see it. His account of the evening claims that he

160

clumsily crawled over the four rows of seating that separated him from the balcony on the front row of the stalls and, leaning over into the space ahead, shouted a single word in the direction of the stage. The word was delivered with as much force as he could express it, but no one could hear it for the din of panic and fear.

The word was deceit.

I am not proud to say that I do not entirely believe this to be true; that his reasoning adjusted to the fact of the matter with ungodly speed, and that acuity arrived at him so exactly.

But then I do not know, and will never know, quite what it was that Mr. Jacob Finlay saw on the stage that terrible night – his account tells us only that it was magnificent – and how it came to be that he would live, when some two hundred souls would die, that night of 13th February 1856, when the fire came to the Pavilion Theatre on Whitechapel Road.

I offer my apology to you, reader. I believe I owe you extrapolation of many things yet to come, and that these things, in turn, owe you a more wholesome understanding of the man that was Jacob Finlay. I wish to tell how it was that Jacob himself, albeit with a little help from his acquaintance, Mr. Alan John Frye, built his own wooden box for great purpose. And I wish to say why it was that he came to found the Committee of the Unfathomable some forty-three years later in London, which would seek to investigate and expose the curious cases of illusion which mask, with intention, something that is not spiritual.

That will come in time, for I know that the grandest illusion was the man himself. My pocket watch talks to me of a late and tiring evening, and soon I must rest. Tomorrow I shall speak on what remained one of Jacob's longest-standing obsessions, one created long before the Committee. For thirteen years, my friend sought to illuminate the truth as he saw it, of what was the substance of the thing known commonly as the African burial trick. His notes reveal his personal witness to one-hundred and six performances of it, conducted as far and as wide as Port Elizabeth, at the southern tip of the African Continent, to Tunis, only a gasp

161

away from the Italian coast. I am certain that Jacob took delight in his obsessive interrogation of each performance.

All were discovered to be fraud, except one.

Harper Channing doesn't take any chances. He's is in pretty good shape for a man that nearly died twice.

Over his sixty-eight years, Harper has been fortunate enough to enjoy a number of paths – as an animator, a journalist, a magician, a child, a clockmaker, a speech writer.

He now blends what little he knows into stories.

He is under no illusion.

His first full-length novel, One, is coming in late 2020.

Thank you

Thank you for purchasing the second volume in the Dark London Anthology.

All royalties received will be split and donated to two London-based charities, The London Community Foundation, and Centrepoint.

The publisher is grateful to those who have contributed to the publication of the Anthology. Their work has been done without payment.

Please consider purchasing Volume One in the Dark London Anthology – available in paperback and on Kindle across Amazon.

Fantastic Books
Great Authors

darkstroke is
an imprint of
Crooked Cat Books

- Gripping Thrillers
- Cosy Mysteries
- Romantic Chick-Lit
- Fascinating Historicals
- Exciting Fantasy
- Young Adult Adventures
- Non-Fiction

Discover us online
www.darkstroke.com

Find us on instagram:
www.instagram.com/darkstrokebooks